The Last Days of Tolstoy

Vladimir Chertkov

The Last Days of Tolstoy

The present edition is a reproduction of previous publication of this classic work. Minor typographical errors may have been corrected without note, however, for an authentic reading experience the spelling, punctuation, and capitalization have been retained from the original text.

ISBN: 978-1-64799-192-0

CONTENTS

INTRODUCTION

Public opinion demands that facts with regard to Tolstoy's going away should be revealed—The conditions of Tolstoy's life were a test of his consistency—Why is it necessary to publish the circumstances of his going away?—The importance of Tolstoy's example—Misrepresentation of the causes of his going away—The moral duty of his friends to defend his memory—My task

PART I

PART II
WHY TOLSTOY WENT AWAY

CHAPTER I
THE CONDITIONS OF LIFE AT YASNAYA POLYANA

Wealthy surroundings—False position in the eyes of men—Spiritual break with his wife

CHAPTER II
CHANGE FOR THE WORSE IN HIS WIFE'S ATTITUDE TO HIM

Change for the worse in the conditions of life at Yasnaya with regard to the management of the estate, to the relations with

CHAPTER III
THE HISTORY OF THE WILL

CHAPTER IV
INTERVALS OF REST—IN OTHER PEOPLE'S HOUSES

CHAPTER V
THE LAST PERIOD

CHAPTER VI
MENTAL AGONY

CHAPTER VII
THE NIGHT OF TOLSTOY'S GOING AWAY

CHAPTER VIII
TOLSTOY'S RELATION TO HIS WIFE

CHAPTER IX
THE MOTIVES THAT DECIDED HIS GOING AWAY

CHAPTER X
THE SIGNIFICANCE OF TOLSTOY'S GOING AWAY AND OF THE WHOLE SPIRITUAL ACHIEVEMENT OF HIS LIFE

PART III
TOLSTOY'S ATTITUDE TO HIS SUFFERINGS

The growth of his inner consciousness during the second period of his life. Extracts from the diary for 1884—Differences with his wife—On the border of despair—Feeling of solitude—Memory of his mother and his longing for her (1906)—Striving after God. Extracts from diary and letters

APPENDIX I

APPENDIX II

INTRODUCTION

So much misunderstanding, misrepresentation, partiality and personal prejudice has accumulated in connection with the last years and days of Leo Nikolaevitch Tolstoy's life, that before starting upon this first detailed account of his "going away" I find myself compelled, at the risk of wearying the reader's patience, to begin with a somewhat lengthy introduction.

Now that Tolstoy's wife[1] is dead, the chief obstacle to revealing the true causes of his going away from Yasnaya Polyana is removed. Like other friends of Leo Nikolaevitch, I have said nothing for ten years. During this time many people, some of them particularly deserving of confidence and respect, have asked me to publish all that I know about this event. As an instance I will quote a letter

---

[1] Sofya Andreyevna Tolstoy, who died in November, 1919. In Appendix II, at the end of the present volume, I explain what attitude towards Sofya Andreyevna I adopt in the present narrative.

from Mrs. Mayo, a well-known English authoress and admirer of Tolstoy.[2]

"Old Aberdeen,
Scotland,
Jan. 17, 1914.

"Dear Mr. Tchertkoff,

"Some of us in Great Britain feel that the time has come when it is highly desirable that we should hear the story of the tragedy which beset the last years of Leo Tolstoy's life, from one who was in its scene.

"We can understand and respect your reticence up to this point. But now so many rumours, derogatory to Tolstoy, and therefore likely to diminish the weight of his teaching, are spreading over the world, and seem to be the subject of a very active propaganda even in this country.

"Hitherto, however, we have heard little or nothing save from those who were notoriously out of sympathy with his principles, and who did not scruple to put obstacles in the way of the carrying out of his last will.

"Further, it has been unfortunate that the Life of Tolstoy best known in Britain is the work of one who, far from being a disciple, is not even a neutral or impartial recorder, but is in flat antagonism to Tolstoy's leading principle of non-resistance to evil by violence.

"Therefore we appeal to you, Tolstoy's personal friend

---

[2] Isabella Fyvie Mayo.

and fellow-worker, that you should let us hear the facts of the case as you saw them.

"Some of us feel that Tolstoy's own works explain enough. I remember when I read the last page of the paper 'Living and Dying,' in his Three Days in the Village, written only a few months before his death, I realised that Tolstoy's spiritual anguish was being strained almost beyond endurance.

"Again, I repeat that we all deeply respect the reticence you have hitherto maintained. But there is a time to speak and a time to keep silent. History shows us again and again how impossible it is to unearth the truth when eye-witnesses are gone. Thus are engendered the most misleading and mischievous myths.

"I trust that you will give this matter your deepest consideration, and I remain,

"Yours with much regard,
(Mrs.) "Isabella Fyvie Mayo."

I have received many such requests, both spoken and written, from many different people, some of whom were noted for their tact and reserve, and whose opinion therefore carried special weight in this delicate matter. Nevertheless I could not make up my mind.

I feel that the time has come at last to speak openly of what I know. I approach my task with no light heart, but with a full consciousness of the moral responsibility which it involves. In doing so I have but one wish: to say nothing that is superfluous or out of date, and to keep back nothing which I feel it my duty to Leo Nikolaevitch and to other people to reveal.

In Leo Nikolaevitch Tolstoy's life two circumstances deserve special notice. In the first place, the immediate external conditions in which he was placed—that is, all he had to endure in his family life and home surroundings—seemed to be specially designed as a severe trial for him. If someone wanted to put to a practical test Leo Nikolaevitch's sincerity, consistency and spiritual strength in carrying out his conception of life, he could not have placed him in conditions more suited for the purpose than those in which Leo Nikolaevitch lived for the last thirty years of his life. Secondly, it is remarkable that Leo Nikolaevitch bore this trial irreproachably, though it was more severe than anyone unacquainted with his intimate life could suppose.

There was a time when all educated Russians imagined, in their spiritual blindness, that Tolstoy's "easy" life in Yasnaya Polyana was a fresh example of the inconsistency with which great thinkers fail to apply to themselves the lofty truths they preach. Tolstoy's enemies rejoiced, and regarded his supposed inconsistency as a proof of his theory being inapplicable in practice. His friends found extenuating circumstances for his guilt, and thought that we should be grateful to Tolstoy for the spiritual food he had given us, and not be too hard upon his human weaknesses. And yet during all this time, with a firmness which nothing could shake, and sometimes at the cost of incredible suffering, Leo Nikolaevitch was carrying on the most heroic work of self-abnegation, consistency and self-restraint of which man is capable. He realised in his actions and in all his personal life that which he preached, and both in his life and his death he exemplified the complete renunciation of all personal desires and the whole-hearted service of God, in which he believed the purpose and the meaning of human life to consist.

I am well aware that this assertion may appear to be an exaggeration. Some readers will be inclined to ascribe my words to the natural enthusiasm of a "Tolstoyan" for his "teacher." Fortunately, however, I have at my disposal a wealth of documentary material which irrefutably confirms the truth of my words. I hope, in due time, to publish this material as well as my own observations and facts known to me with regard to Leo Nikolaevitch's family life as a whole.

Written documents which I have in my keeping sufficiently reveal the general character of the conditions in which Leo Nikolaevitch had to live. But if there were only these data to go upon, one would have to resign oneself to inevitable blanks and omissions. The readers would have to treat these documents like learned investigators treat their historical material—that is, to fill up the blanks with their own surmises, to connect the disconnected, and to reconcile contradictions in accordance with their personal predilections and the degree of their inventiveness. Among the extensive material relating to Tolstoy's life there already exist, and will no doubt appear in the future, communications which more or less misrepresent the facts and even contain downright falsehoods. To the malicious joy of Tolstoy's enemies there has already accumulated a whole literature which depicts his personality, his life, his "going away" and his death in a totally perverted manner, and is full of shameless slander.

Under such circumstances, the future biographers of Tolstoy would have—as is usually the case—to steer a middle course between all the contradictory data in their possession. In doing so they will not be able to avoid the misleading influence of the unreliable documents—and this, indeed, is already noticeable in some of the recent biographies. In view of this, it is particularly important that some contemporary of Tolstoy who was particularly intimate with him, enjoyed his full confidence and had a first-hand knowledge of the true conditions of his home life, should leave a consecutive exposition of all the relevant and well-authenticated facts. It is desirable, too, that this person should not be one of Tolstoy's relatives, and would therefore be free from all family prejudices and predilections.

Not in virtue of any personal merits, but only owing to certain external circumstances, I satisfy these conditions, and cannot help feeling that fate itself lays upon me the moral duty of undertaking such a work.

A detailed account is necessary not only for the sake of "historical accuracy" in the biography of the great man; it is needed in the interests of humanity in order to preserve in all its intact wholeness the striking example of Tolstoy's life; for this life incontestably proves the possibility of carrying out in practice the lofty truths to which he gave verbal expression.

It would be a mistake to agree with only such truths as are proclaimed by men who perfectly realise in the practice of their own lives that which they preach. It is part of our nature that a man may be clearly conscious of truths so lofty that it is beyond his power to put them into practice. They may be practised by his contemporaries who have more strength than he has, or by future generations who will have attained a higher degree of moral perfection. But it is also part of our nature that the example of a man who realises in his own conduct, in spite of any privations and suffering, and even at the cost of his life, that which he preaches, always arouses the enthusiastic sympathy of others, and becomes a powerful help and encouragement to many who strive to follow the ideals proclaimed by such a man.

Even if in his personal life Tolstoy were inconsistent and failed to live up to his own convictions, he would still deserve our profound gratitude for the enormous, immeasurable impetus which, by his intellectual work, he has given to the development of human consciousness. But it has pleased destiny to create in the person of Tolstoy not only a thinker of genius, but also a man of great moral heroism. It is therefore very important to preserve the most exact information about his personal life, especially about that side of it which called for most self-sacrifice on his part and made him suffer most in carrying out his principles in practice. Finally, I was led to undertake the present work by my personal relation to Leo Nikolaevitch. Our intimate friendship of many years' standing, my ardent devotion and love for him in his lifetime, and now my devotion to his memory, infinitely dear to me, my respect and reverence for the Divine Principle which expressed itself in him with such power and purity—all make me eager to do my utmost to preserve for men in all its striking, untarnished brilliance the truth about the greatness of his moral achievement. Since there are people to whom this truth is unpleasant or damaging, and who seek to pervert or conceal it in every way, making wild inventions about Leo Nikolaevitch, or demanding that truth shall not be revealed, surely it behoves his most intimate friends to champion his memory and preserve his noble image from pollution or distortion.

Now that Leo Nikolaevitch's widow, for whose sake we have refrained from publishing the facts, is no longer alive, it is not only permissible for us, his friends, to come forward in his defence but, in view of all that has happened, it is our bounden duty to tell the truth about his life and death, so as to counteract all the slanders that have been set going by his enemies.[3]

---

[3] In this connection I venture to quote here a small extract from my article entitled "Should the truth about Tolstoy's going away be told?" (published in the magazine Tolstoy's Voice and Unity, N 3 (15)).

"The conditions under which Leo Nikolaevitch Tolstoy left Yasnaya Polyana and died on the journey at a railway station were, as everyone knows, quite exceptional. And yet, though it happened ten years ago, mankind does not to this day know the true causes of this event. Both in Russia and abroad the actual reasons that drove a man like Leo Tolstoy to leave his family are unknown, and so everyone invented his own reasons and published all sorts of fictions. Some have maintained that Tolstoy longed to be received once more into the Orthodox Church and wanted to save his soul in a monastery. Some insisted that as he grew old his intellect grew so weak that he did not know what he was doing, and, instinctively feeling the approach of death, went off without any definite purpose. Others observed with satisfaction that at the end of his life, at any rate, Tolstoy succeeded in overcoming his attachment to his family and his bondage to wealthy surroundings, and in doing what in accordance with his convictions he ought to have done long ago. Others, on the contrary, regretted that he had not the strength to endure the trials of his home life to the end, and that, revolted at the behaviour of his family, he lost his spiritual balance and failed in his duty to his relatives. There is no enumerating all the guesses and suppositions that were spread by people who attempted during the last ten years to solve the riddle of Tolstoy's 'going away,' or who intentionally perverted the truth. Quite recently in his book on Tolstoy (which has already been translated into foreign languages), Maxim Gorky, with his usual amazing rashness in dealing with subjects which he does not know or fails to understand, thought it fit, by the side of other absurdities about Tolstoy, to inform the world that Leo Nikolaevitch left Yasnaya Polyana 'with the despotic intention of increasing the oppressive influence of his religious ideas' and 'compelling people to accept them,' and that he, Maxim Gorky, does not approve of such behaviour.

"I owe it to my friend's memory to show how ill-grounded are the accusations and the slanders with which men, misinformed as to the circumstances of his life, or opposed to his theories, tried to besmirch his name. I naturally want to do my utmost to reinstate in all its beauty and

I have also heard another argument from persons who would have preferred, for the sake of their vanity, that Tolstoy's family tragedy should have remained secret. They said that Leo Nikolaevitch himself never defended himself against those who slandered him. He preferred to bear the censure of public opinion rather than reveal the painful conditions of his life and allow others to be blamed instead of himself. And therefore, they say, after his death his friends ought to follow his example.

It is impossible to agree with this. One may well understand that Leo Nikolaevitch concealed his sufferings. He drew strength and derived satisfaction from the consciousness that he was living not before men, but before God. Far from standing in need of human approbation, he thought that unjust condemnation on the part of men was good for him in so far as it forcibly drove him to that road upon which one has nothing but the voice of God in one's own soul for guidance. But does this mean that we too must say nothing about Tolstoy's heroic life and conceal his moral rectitude now, when he is not among us?

We have not, cannot have, and ought not to have, the same motives which in this respect influenced him. It is good for me, for my soul, to be unjustly condemned owing to the fact that I do not want to justify myself and am sparing the real culprit. But there is nothing good in my being silent when another person is unjustly condemned or slandered in my presence, while I have the means of proving his innocence. Leo Nikolaevitch had grounds for not justifying himself before men; but we have no grounds whatever for concealing that which does justify him. In the present case we ought to be guided, not by the thought of ourselves in his place if

purity the spiritual image of him to whom I am indebted so much for his love and moral assistance."

he were alive, but by the immediate voice of our own heart and reason, which demands that we should defend the friend whose memory is being reviled before our eyes.

These are the reasons that have led me to undertake the biographical work of which the present narrative of Tolstoy's going away forms, so to speak, only one separate chapter.

All the events of cosmic life are so inextricably interwoven that, were it possible to change in the past some one of them, even the apparently most insignificant, it would be necessary to change at the same time absolutely all the other concurrent and preceding circumstances. Therefore in order to investigate fully the conditions which have occasioned this or that event in a person's life, one would have to consider the whole past history of mankind, both the external and the internal or spiritual. And since it is impossible even in thought to embrace all this infinite number of facts, it must be admitted that it is utterly beyond our power to determine all the causes that have produced this or that event in the life of a particular individual.

Thus in the story of Tolstoy's "going away" which occupies us now, no investigation, however careful, can exhaust all the outer and inner circumstances, receding into an endless past, that have brought about the event in question. Besides, even in the domain of Tolstoy's personal life which admits of inquiry, the direct and indirect causes of his "going away" are so numerous and many-sided that it is beyond the power of a single individual to make an exhaustive enumeration of them. The colouring given in such cases to the circumstances under investigation and the very drift of the inquiry depend so largely upon the personal point of view and the mood of the writer, that, try as he may to be impartial, his selection and treatment of causes will inevitably be more or less one-sided.

Therefore in order to bring to light the causes of Tolstoy's "going away," it is extremely important that the greatest possible number of his contemporaries should record and preserve for future generations the facts known to them as well as their thoughts and reminiscences; and it is desirable, too, that this should be done particularly by those of them who had occasion to stand nearest to Tolstoy's personal and family life. A true history of Tolstoy's life must be preserved in the greatest possible fullness for future generations. His contemporaries, and in the first place his relatives, personal friends and co-workers, ought not to neglect this important task laid upon them by fate itself.

So far as I am concerned, I quite realise that the small beginning which I venture to make with the present narrative is only a drop in the sea of all the facts, observations and deductions which it would be desirable to gather together before Tolstoy's contemporaries leave the scene of this earthly life.[4]

In composing the present book I have tried to distinguish as sharply as possible between: (1) facts and circumstances which I knew for certain, and therefore have stated them without any reservations; (2) facts and circumstances of the certainty of which I personally am convinced, though I do not consider myself entitled to affirm them unconditionally, and state them with some reservations; (3) circumstances surmised by me on the ground of certain data which I quote herewith; and (4) my personal opinions, considerations and reflections upon the facts quoted.

Being compelled in the present narrative to be as brief as possible, I

---

[4] In connection with the Tolstoy Museum in Moscow (Pretchistenka 11) a circle has been formed with the object, partly, of collecting and preserving such communications. Some of them may, with the author's consent, be published in the Viestnik.

am unable to substantiate all my assertions by documentary and other evidence in my possession. I am therefore addressing myself here only to such readers who can take my word for it that I give out as facts only that which is known to me for certain, and do not permit myself any embellishments or exaggeration. But in the other, still unwritten, book to which I have referred, Tolstoy's Moral Achievement, the subject of his family life as a whole will be extensively treated and I shall quote my data in full.

If I often permit myself to include in the narrative my personal valuation of the events, this is certainly not because I want to force my own opinions on the reader instead of barely stating the facts and letting him draw his own conclusions. I quite recognise the advantages of a so-called objective narrative, but it was not what in the present case I had in view. As I have mentioned already, my purpose in writing this book was to contradict the slanders against Leo Nikolaevitch and the misinterpretations of his conduct. I do not doubt that the majority of my readers will consider my selection of facts and my interpretation of them one-sided. Let, then, other investigators of the same subject interpret the facts each from his own point of view. The more such narratives are published, the less risk there will be of the reader receiving a one-sided impression, and the more free he will be to draw his own conclusions.

As to a detailed objective exposition of all the circumstances connected with Tolstoy's "going away," I believe that, desirable as it is, the time for it has not yet come, for the persons who possess most information on the subject have not yet had time to publish the numerous and varied details known to them. Let us hope that they will not put off this task for so long that they will be dead before they have fulfilled it. And if my present contribution will induce them also to give out something of what they know, even if it were solely with the object of contradicting me, I should be very glad of it, as indeed of any corrections of my work that anyone might wish to make. It is far better that the matter should be thoroughly thrashed out between the eye-witnesses rather than—as often happens with the lives of distinguished men—it should become, in future ages, the subject of an extensive polemic literature which seldom succeeds in getting at truth. It seems to me that only when there appear the greatest possible number of additional communications on the same subject shall we be able to work out, from all the accumulated material, that really objective and trustworthy account of Tolstoy's "going away" which is so necessary in order to give men a true idea of the spiritual achievement of his life.

V. Tchertkoff
Moscow, Lefortovsky pereulok, 7
January 1922

PART I

WHY TOLSTOY DID NOT LEAVE HIS HOME

(From a letter to H. Dosev, October 19, 1910[5])

Dear Dosev,

I feel that I must protest against what you say in your last letter in connection with Leo Nikolaevitch.

Among other things you say of him: "Nothing is worse than slavery. And worse still is slavery to a spoilt child who has been

---

[5] Ten days before Leo Nikolaevitch went away from Yasnaya Polyana this letter was written by me to Christo Dosev, the common friend of Tolstoy and myself, who migrated to Russia from Bulgaria and died in the year 1919. I quote my letter word for word to preserve its direct character. I ought to mention that a few years after Tolstoy's death Dosev told me that he recognised how mistaken was the censure of Tolstoy to which he had given expression in the letter which called forth this answer from me.

spoilt by oneself. But I know nothing worse in the world than being enslaved to an irrational, self-willed woman who is convinced that her slave husband will do whatever she chooses. Is not Sofya Andreyevna such a woman, and is not Leo Nikolaevitch in slavery to her? His submissiveness to Sofya Andreyevna I regard not as a virtue but as a weakness. He makes concessions to her through fear of sinning against love; but in doing this is he not sinning against the great love? You know she keeps him away from his friends, from the peasants, from humanity; she makes him live the revolting life of a wealthy landowner. I do not reproach Leo Nikolaevitch, I do not condemn him—I love and respect him too much. But I am sorry for him. I am sorry for his whole life, and for his great teaching, which has not passed in vain for himself and for those near him, but which will pass in vain for the peasants and for humanity; for his external life blurs all the significance and meaning of his words and thoughts in men's eyes."

You conclude with the words: "Do not be hurt by my words. I repeat—this is the expression not of censure, but of the pain of a man who loves him. And so if there is something I don't see rightly, you and all the others and Leo Nikolaevitch must forgive me. The greatest joy of my life is my love for him and for all of you, friends of the spirit."

Just because I believe in the sincerity of your love for Leo Nikolaevitch, and know that he too loves you, just because of that I feel irresistibly impelled to answer those words of yours, dear friend. You really do not "see rightly," and are mistaken in assuming slavishness and inconsistency in Leo Nikolaevitch. On the contrary, he displays in his attitude to Sofya Andreyevna the greatest freedom—freedom from anxiety about the opinion of men, and the highest consistency—the determination to do, according to

2

the measure of his powers and understanding, not his own will but the will of God. And for the sake of doing this will of God he is ready to endure any personal sufferings of his own and any human censure and disgrace.

You are mistaken in supposing that Leo Nikolaevitch does whatever Sofya Andreyevna wishes. On the contrary, there is a limit beyond which he does not give way to her. He does not give way to her when she demands from him what is distinctly against his conscience. And it is just because he does not give way entirely, but adheres to this limit in his concessions—it is just through that, that he has so much to put up with from Sofya Andreyevna.

During the last ten years of his life Leo Nikolaevitch has often thought of leaving his wife, and has more than once been on the verge of taking that step. It is still perfectly possible that he will take it in the end if he becomes convinced that his remaining with his wife is not attaining his object, but merely exciting her, and encouraging her in her exactingness and tyranny. But to do this he must clearly and unmistakably recognise in his conscience that he ought to leave her. That he has not hitherto left her is not at all because it is more agreeable or more convenient to live in her house, it is not at all through weakness of character or dread of disobeying her; but, believe me, solely because he is not yet sufficiently convinced that he ought to go away, and does not feel that it is God's will that he should go. For him personally it would be so much more agreeable, peaceful and in every way convenient to go away, that he is afraid of acting selfishly, of doing what is easier for himself, and of refusing through cowardice to bear the trials laid upon him.

If he did leave Yasnaya Polyana at his advanced age, and with his infirmities, he could not now live by manual labour. Nor could he go staff in hand about the world and fall ill and die somewhere by the high-road, or as a passing pilgrim in a peasant's hut. He could not do it simply from affection for those who love him, for his daughters and the friends who are near him in heart and spirit— however attractive such an end might be for him himself, and however theatrically splendid it might seem to the crowd which at present censures him. He could not without being cruel refuse to settle in some modest abode where, without the help of servants, they could do his housework for him, surrounding him with the affection and care necessary at his age, giving him the opportunity of associating without hindrance with the working people whom he loves so much, and from whom he is at present completely cut off. Why, such a free, quiet life would be a real paradise for him in comparison with the prison in which he has to live now!

It will be asked why he does not accept for himself these happy surroundings so easily within his reach, seeing that his wife has, one would have thought, given him long ago sufficient ground for leaving her house. Why does he not now, at least, in the decline of his age, cast off the heavy burden which in the person of Sofya Andreyevna he has been bearing on his shoulders for thirty years, sometimes almost sinking under its weight? It is obvious that if he does not do this it is not from weakness or cowardice, and it is not from selfishness; but, on the contrary, from a feeling of duty, from a manly determination to remain at his post to the very end, sacrificing his preferences and his personal happiness for the sake of doing what he considers to be the divine will.

In July, 1908, Leo Nikolaevitch passed through one of those agonising spiritual crises, provoked by Sofya Andreyevna, which with him nearly always ended in serious illness. So it was on this occasion. Immediately after it he fell ill, and for some time after it

4

was almost at death's door. I quote a few extracts from his diary in the days just before his illness.

"*July 2, 1908.*—If I had heard of myself as an outsider—of a man living in luxury, wringing all he can out of the peasants, locking them up in prison, while preaching and professing Christianity and giving away coppers, and for all his loathsome actions sheltering himself behind his dear wife, I should not hesitate to call him a blackguard! And that is just what I need that I may be set free from the praises of men and live for my soul....

"*July 2, 1908.*—Doubts have come into my mind whether I do right to be silent, and even whether it would not be better for me to go away, to disappear. I refrain from doing this principally because it would be for my own sake, in order to escape from a life poisoned on every side. I believe that the endurance of this life is needful for me....

"*July 3, 1908.*—It is still as agonising, life here in Yasnaya Polyana is completely poisoned. Wherever I turn, it is shame and suffering....

"*July 6, 1908.*—Help me, O Lord! Again I long to go away, and I do not make up my mind to; but do not give up the idea. The great point is: whether I would be doing it for my own sake if I went away. That I am not doing it for my own sake in staying I know....

"*July 9, 1908.*—One thing grows more and more agonising; the injustice of the senseless luxury in the midst of which I am living with undeserved poverty and want all around. I feel worse and worse, more and more wretched. I cannot forget, I cannot help seeing...."

I remember on one of these days Leo Nikolaevitch returning from a

5

solitary walk in the woods with that expression of joyful inspiration which so often illumined his face of late years, and meeting me with the words:

"I have been thinking a great deal and very deeply. And it has become so clear to me that when one stands at the parting of the ways and does not know how to act, one ought always to give the preference to the decision which involves more self-sacrifice."

From all this it is evident how deeply Leo Nikolaevitch feels his position, how passionately he longs at times to throw off his yoke and at the same time with what sincerity and self-sacrifice he is seeking not his own comfort, but only one thing—the clear understanding of how he ought to act before his conscience, before his God, to whose service he had devoted his life not in word alone but in deed also.

After this how short-sighted, how unjust and cruel seem utterances—especially on the lips of a loved and loving friend of Leo Nikolaevitch's, as you are—such as that you look upon his submission to Sofya Andreyevna not as a virtue but as a weakness. We may suppose that in Leo Nikolaevitch's place we should act differently, though it would be difficult for us to say whether in so acting we should be doing better or worse than he. We cannot understand all that is passing in his soul, and so we may be perplexed by some of his actions. But I at least cannot help feeling the greatest respect for the pure, self-sacrificing impulses by which he is guided. I cannot help feeling complete confidence in him on this question, for if anyone, sacrificing all his personal needs and pleasures, and regardless of his suffering and privations, whatever they may be, tries unswervingly to follow the dictates of his conscience, he is doing all that can be expected of a human being, and no one has the right to condemn, nor need anyone be anxious

6

about him. You see, for us, looking on Leo Nikolaevitch's life from outside, it appears in reality as an external phenomenon which we can consider according to our mood. In our moments of leisure we venture to criticise Leo Nikolaevitch and his manner of life and to decide on its value, as though it were far easier for us to grasp and understand it, than it is for him. "Another man's trouble I can handle easily, but my own is beyond my comprehension." We forget that for us it is only a subject of criticism about which we may have one opinion or another—a question concerning which we may on occasion argue and bring forward the pros and cons. But for Leo Nikolaevitch it is a question of conscience, it is the very business of his life, it is that into which he is putting all his soul, all his understanding. What grounds have we for imagining that we outsiders, who know ourselves to be greatly inferior to Leo Nikolaevitch spiritually, are capable of understanding his life better and deciding more conscientiously for him how he ought to act than he can himself, though he is seeking guidance for his conduct day and night before God?

Let his enemies vent their malice over his seemingly humiliating position; let narrow-minded and short-sighted "Tolstoyans," who have neither spiritual penetration nor the delicate intuition of the heart, condemn him or bestow their patronising pity on him; but we, his real friends, who are of one spirit with him, who understand by what he is living, and are struggling towards the same goal as he, we, dear Dosev, ought to have more faith and trust in him.

As you are aware, none of Leo Nikolaevitch's friends suffers more from Leo Nikolaevitch's relations with Sofya Andreyevna than my wife and I, for they deprive us of one of the greatest joys of our life—of personal intercourse with him, the enjoyment of which was the principal reason for our settling in this district.[6] But when I am in a good frame of mind, all this which is painful and humiliating vanishes before my trust in Leo Nikolaevitch, and my conviction, which nothing will shake, that he desires nothing for himself, but is striving for one thing only—that is, that at every given moment he may be doing what God requires of him.

Some members of his household who are devoted to Leo Nikolaevitch are distressed that he should give in to the farce—to them obvious—which Sofya Andreyevna so often plays before him in order to attain her objects, at one time agitating him by feigned attacks of despair and frenzy, at other times touching his heart by displays of penitence, meekness and care for his welfare which are even more insincere, or, if at times half sincere, are at least extremely transitory. But it seems to me that if, through the wonderful purity of his own heart, Leo Nikolaevitch is incapable of seeing Sofya Andreyevna as she really is, and with touching trustfulness seizes upon every justification for recognising in her the smallest signs of an awakening conscience, then, though he may be mistaken in it, the tender emotion and joy which he feels on such occasions are perfectly legitimate, because they arise from his great love and readiness to forgive everything. It is doubtful whether her success in pretending is good for Sofya Andreyevna herself. But who knows, perhaps this wonderful faith in her soul on the part of Leo Nikolaevitch, which nothing can shake, his continual expectation, his premature, eager anticipation of the spiritual awakening in her which he so whole-heartedly desires, will in due

---

[6] This letter was written at the time when, though living only a few versts from Yasnaya Polyana, I was forcibly separated from Leo Nikolaevitch. This separation, which lasted for about three months, was due to the hostile attitude towards me of his wife, whose excited condition he hoped to soothe by the promise not to see me.

time have its effect upon Sofya Andreyevna. Perhaps such an attitude to her on the part of the man whom she has so mercilessly tortured for so many years, and who nevertheless is of all people the only one who has sincerely loved her, and loved her to the end, will one day be reflected in her soul. The memory of this in its due time, for instance, when she will become conscious of the nearness of her own death, when all worldly plans, aims and desires inevitably retreat into the background, is the one thing that may be capable of awakening in that unhappy woman the divine spark, the possibility of which we have no right to deny in any human being. And if this is possible, is it surprising that Leo Nikolaevitch, entirely given up to the service of the divine love as he is, should untiringly attempt to melt with his love the heart of the partner of his life whom he once drew to himself, with whom he shared his past sinful life, and with whom he would also wish to save his soul?

And indeed as a rule, dear Dosev, I am deeply convinced that no one of us can decide for another, nor determine in regard to another man's behaviour what is his weakness and what is his virtue. "Before his God," as it is written in the gospel, "every one of us shall stand or fall." It is not for us human beings to meddle in the secret region of another man's soul with our short-sighted criticisms, our frivolous verdicts and our mistaken condolences.

And however Leo Nikolaevitch may act in the future—whether he remains to the end beside his wife, or whether at some time he finds it necessary for her benefit to go away from her—I am convinced of one thing: that in that matter he will really act only as his conscience bids him, and therefore he will act rightly.

Why, if Leo Nikolaevitch's wife were drowning and, plunging into the water to save her, he perished himself, nobody would reproach

9

him for having sacrificed his friends and humanity for the sake of excessive family attachments. It is even more impossible to reproach him for devoting his life, sacrificing its joys and repose, and perhaps even giving it up altogether, for the sake of saving his wife from the ruin of her soul.

It ought not to be forgotten also that at the same time Leo Nikolaevitch always contrives in the most attentive and sensitive way to respond to every real need, spiritual or material, of the whole people and of all mankind, devoting his whole working time to intense spiritual labour in the interests of the working masses, and of all suffering mankind, whether the suffering be from external or internal evil.

As for your idea that for the simple people and for humanity "all his life and great teaching will pass in vain, because his external life blurs all the significance and meaning of his words and thoughts in men's eyes," on this too, I assure you, you are profoundly mistaken.

His words cannot pass in vain for humanity if only from the fact that they do not express something of "his own" with which only those who "follow him" can agree, but express the best that there is in the heart of every man. And from that very fact what Tolstoy says in his writings finds, apart from any relation to his own personal life, a direct and loving response in the heart and consciousness of all men whose conscience has not been blunted. And as time passes this response will only become clearer and more distinct.

When the true conditions of the domestic life of Leo Nikolaevitch become generally known, the great heroism of his family life, reproducing in deed what he expressed in words, will be added to the direct persuasive force of his words in the eyes of humanity.

"Going to the people," to prison, torture, the cross, the stake, the scaffold—all these have been already. And however deserving of the deepest respect are the men who face these for conscience' sake, yet if it is a question of a living example, we, people of the present day, needed an example of yet another kind.

Men go willingly to the scaffold even from a desire to blow their neighbour into the air. Men become cripples for life or are killed for the sake of beating a record with a motor-car or an aeroplane. All this is striking and sensational, but already no one is surprised by it. But it is quite a different matter to spend several decades with such a wife as Sofya Andreyevna without running away from her, and still preserving in his heart pity and love for her, and this to the accompaniment of the unceasing mockery of his enemies and misunderstanding and censure from the majority of his friends—so to live from day to day, from year to year, not seeing and not foreseeing any escape but his own death; to endure, in doing so, all that Leo Nikolaevitch has to endure, being periodically made ill by it and almost dying, and not only to have not the smallest blame or bitterness in his heart, but, on the contrary, to be always blaming himself for lack of patience and love—this really is the highest consistency on the part of Leo Nikolaevitch. This is a testimony of the truthfulness of his theory of life than which nothing stronger and more striking could be imagined. This is just the example that humanity is in need of in our day, and this example Leo Nikolaevitch is giving us in his life.

When one looks at the matter from this point of view it becomes so clear as to be obvious why Leo Nikolaevitch had to have just such a wife as was vouchsafed to him. "For a great ship a great journey." He who delivered the message of love in its absolutely unlimited

11

sense needed to have the possibility in his life of proving in action that a love that nothing in the world could destroy was really attainable for man. And in due time, when the truth about Leo Nikolaevitch's life becomes common property, men will be infinitely grateful to him for this joyous confirmation of the possibility of following in practice the godly theory of life of which Tolstoy is the exponent in his writings.

PART II

WHY TOLSTOY WENT AWAY

CHAPTER I

LIFE AT YASNAYA POLYANA

A few days after the foregoing letter was written Leo Nikolaevitch left Yasnaya Polyana.

At first sight it may seem that if he did well in remaining so long with his wife, he ought not to have abandoned her in the end; or, on the contrary, if he was right in going away, it was a mistake not to have done so sooner.

That is how many do reason. Some—the majority—commend him for his departure, considering that thereby he "atoned" for his

13

supposed weakness and inconsistency in the past. Others—a small minority—commend him, on the contrary, for remaining so many years with his wife, but consider his going away a proof of his inconsistency.[7]

It seems to me that in any case Leo Nikolaevitch's friends who were able to estimate at its true value the self-sacrifice with which he remained a voluntary prisoner in his wife's house for so many years ought, more than anyone, to have that confidence in him of which he was worthy. They might at least be confident that if, after all this, he did decide to go away, he must have had good grounds for doing so; especially since such an explanation is far more natural and credible than the supposition that Leo Nikolaevitch, who had so successfully endured this prolonged ordeal and had displayed such striking stoicism and self-sacrifice, on the eve of his death suddenly, for some reason, broke down and was false to his conscience.

In regard to the question of whether he was to remain with his wife or go away, Leo Nikolaevitch was guided not by any one impulse, but by many, and often contradictory, impulses.

On the side of not leaving his wife he had various considerations which are touched on in my letter to Dosev. The chief of them was his consciousness that in remaining he was fulfilling the demands

---

[7] I have come across references to my letter to Dosev as though it proved that, for all my devotion to Leo Nikolaevitch, I considered that he ought not to have left his wife. But there is nothing of the sort in my letter, the main drift of which is merely that no one has the right to set himself up as a judge of Leo Nikolaevitch in the matter. I indicated in detail how sound were the reasons impelling him to remain in Yasnaya Polyana while he did remain there; but at the same time, in the very same letter, though it was written before Leo Nikolaevitch went away, I made several allusions to the possibility that in the end he would think it necessary to go.

of love in regard to Sofya Andreyevna, and was trying to do her good, while he was performing an act of self-sacrifice for the benefit of his own soul.

He had also, in the course of the last thirty years of his life, many grounds for going away; and though, until the time was ripe, they could not outweigh those that kept him with his family, yet in themselves they were very weighty.

On one side he was painfully conscious—and ever more painfully as time went on—of all the injustice, all the sinfulness of the surroundings of his home life, which were those of a rich landowner in the midst of the poverty around him, and he never forgave himself for his participation in those surroundings. Some months before his death he wrote, as is well known, in the introduction to his novel, There are No Guilty in the World: "The complicated conditions of the past, my family and its demands, have not let me out of their clutches"; and, at once, with the fear of self-justification characteristic of him, hastened to add "or rather I had not the ability nor strength to free myself from them." But recognising at that time the hopelessness of his position, Leo Nikolaevitch found a good side in the fact that it was so painful to him. "Being without any desire for self-justification, or any fear of the liberated peasants, and also without the peasants' envy and bitterness against their oppressors, I am in the most favourable position for seeing the truth and being able to tell it. Perhaps it was just for this that I have been placed by fate in this strange position. I will try, as far as I know how, to take advantage of it. This at least to some extent, anyway, alleviates my condition."

On the other hand, he was at times much distressed by the consciousness of the false position in which he was placed before men, and before the peasants especially, by the external conditions

15

of his life, which were so directly opposed to his convictions. He was well aware that the majority of people condemned him for taking part in that life. But he was resigned even to that, finding a spiritual blessing in his humiliation before men. In his Circle of Reading[8] he said: "What is called religious folly, i.e. conduct which provokes censure and attack, is intelligible and desirable as the sole proof of one's love for God and one's neighbour." "The condemnation by man of your actions," he says in a private letter, "if your actions are not due to selfish motives, but to doing the will of God, is far from requiring you to justify them; on the contrary, this condemnation is a benefit, in that it gives you certain conviction that you do what you are doing not for the praise of men, but for the sake of your soul, for God."[9]

But above all Leo Nikolaevitch had to suffer directly from his wife's antagonism and disagreement with regard to what was for him more precious than anything. This hostility on the part of his wife often reached the point of unconcealed hatred of him, making him at times despair of the possibility of softening her heart at all. As years went on the spiritual rift between them became complete. Leo Nikolaevitch had periods of such doubt and depression of spirit that he felt quite hopeless, and was ready to run away from home. One of these periods I have referred to above, but even at the beginning of the 'eighties Leo Nikolaevitch had moments when he could scarcely restrain himself from going away.

It was so, for instance, in the summer of the year 1884. In his diary of that time we find such entries: "If only I could have confidence in myself.... I cannot go on with this savage life. Even for them" (the members of his family) "it would be a benefit. They will reconsider

---

[8] Circle of Reading, May 17.
[9] 1907.

things if they have anything like a heart.... I said nothing, but I felt horribly depressed. I went away, and meant to go away altogether, but her being with child made me turn back half way to Tula.... It was horribly painful.... It was a mistake not to go away. I think it will be bound to happen sooner or later."[10]

After 1884, as Leo Nikolaevitch's spiritual forces developed further and gained strength, he did succeed to some extent in bearing patiently the insults and suffering inflicted upon him, and learnt to resign himself to the painfulness of his position, extracting gain for his inner life from all that he endured. But how hard it still was for him may be seen, for instance, from the confession that broke from him in conversation with a friend of his, the peasant M. P. Novikov, when the latter visited him on the 21st October, 1910: "I have never concealed from you that in this house I am boiling as in hell, and I have always dreamed of going away, and longed to go somewhere into the forest to a keeper's hut, or to a village to some lonely peasant's hut, where we could help one another. But God has not given me the strength to break away from my family. My weakness is perhaps a sin, but I could not for the sake of my personal satisfaction make others suffer, even although they are members of my family...."

During this time everything that was painful in Leo Nikolaevitch's relations with Sofya Andreyevna, and which had grown with the decades, began to develop with increased rapidity. In this brief but terribly concentrated period of his life much which his goodwill towards her had prevented him from observing in Sofya Andreyevna before began to be apparent to him. At first it was very difficult for him to see his way in his complicated position and among all the varied feelings and impulses which rose up in his

---

[10] June 17-24, 1884

soul. He had not only to bear his old, long familiar cross, but also to deal with new, quite unforeseen trials before he had time to see clearly what attitude he ought to take up to them.

These exceptionally complicated conditions must be kept in view in order to follow Leo Nikolaevitch's spiritual experiences of that period with any degree of accuracy. It was difficult for him to understand his own state of mind, and he exercised the greatest circumspection in order not to act prematurely nor precipitately. It is all the more necessary for us to be extremely circumspect in examining the various spiritual states which followed each other and were interwoven in him at that time. It is impossible to approach the very complicated workings of his soul with ready-made theories, or to offer a rough-and-ready explanation of Leo Nikolaevitch's behaviour on the lines of one's personal bias— whether domestic, religious, social, or otherwise; and least of all can one be guided by information or argument coming from his domestic circle, whose vanity was so deeply wounded by his departure. In order really to understand Tolstoy and his behaviour in this most important period of his life, it is above all needful to free oneself from the slightest partiality, narrowness and one-sidedness, to be ready to look the truth in the face and as far as possible to weigh attentively all the conditions and circumstances, not taken separately, but in combination and in all their complex interaction.

18

CHAPTER II

CHANGE FOR THE WORSE IN HIS WIFE'S ATTITUDE TO HIM

And so in the last few months before Leo Nikolaevitch left Yasnaya Polyana he was subjected in an intensified form to all the agonising conditions which had for many years made him long to get away from his family. What went on around him in Yasnaya Polyana, particularly in the management of the estate, seemed to be purposely calculated to wound, insult and revolt him more and more in his most sacred feelings. In her relations with the peasants Sofya Andreyevna, far from restraining herself through consideration for her husband, behaved with peculiar injustice and harshness as though to spite him.[11]

---

[11] At the beginning of the eighties of the last century, Leo Nikolaevitch's feeling against property in general, and the ownership of land in particular, began to take shape, though it was only somewhat later that it was fully fixed and confirmed. He renounced all property for himself personally in 1894, acting as though in that respect he were dead, that is,

At one time she would try to impress on the peasants that she was acting with the consent and approval of Leo Nikolaevitch himself; at another she would boast before him that his championship had no influence on her arrangements. It is easy to imagine how unutterably painful all this was for him. It is sufficient to recall how he sobbed when he chanced to come across a policeman on horseback dragging along a Yasnaya Polyana peasant caught in the Tolstoys' forest, an old man whom Leo Nikolaevitch knew well and respected. Fully realising that he would not in the least improve the position of the peasants by going away, Leo Nikolaevitch went on regarding such spectacles as a bitter trial laid upon him, and confining himself to protesting warmly on every possible occasion. In the same way, that is as a trial laid upon him, he continued to look upon the false position in which he was placed in the eyes of the public by his apparent acceptance of what was done in Yasnaya Polyana. On this subject he not only continually received abusive letters which he accepted as a useful exercise in humility, but also from time to time persons wishing him well addressed him with censure and exhortation. A letter written by Leo Nikolaevitch at the beginning of 1910 in answer to an unknown student who had written to persuade him to leave his privileged surroundings, is characteristic:

"Your letter touched me," wrote Leo Nikolaevitch; "what you advise me to do is my cherished dream! That I should be living at home

---

leaving the possession of his former property to those whom he regarded as his heirs, that is, his family. After this Sofya Andreyevna began to manage the estate of Yasnaya Polyana, while his children divided the land and property between them. Later on Leo Nikolaevitch felt, he said, that he had made a mistake in giving up the land to his "heirs" instead of to the local peasants, and at the desire of his family confirming the transfer by legal act.

with my wife and daughter in horrible, shameful conditions of luxury in the midst of the poverty around us tortures me unceasingly and ever more and more; and not a day passes on which I do not think of carrying out your advice."

At the same time a third and most painful trial, consisting in his wife's immediate attitude to him, was intensely accentuated. The mournful recital of those spiritual agonies which shattered his health, and which she systematically inflicted on him in the last months of his life, will be set forth in its time and place. No one can imagine what he had to endure and to suffer at that time. On one occasion, calling in D. P. Makovitsky,[12] Leo Nikolaevitch said to him: "Dushan Petrovitch, go to her" (Sofya Andreyevna) "and tell her that if she desires my death she is going the right way to bring it about."[13] In a touching letter of July 14, 1910, to Sofya Andreyevna, Leo Nikolaevitch, after making her every concession he considered possible, adds in conclusion: "If you will not accept these conditions of a good and peaceful life, then I will go away.... I will certainly go away, because it is impossible to go on living like this."

It will be readily understood that with such a position of affairs Leo Nikolaevitch began to foresee more and more definitely the possibility that in the end he would have to leave Yasnaya Polyana.

In a moment of openness he said to his friend, the peasant Novikov: "Yes, yes, believe me, I tell you frankly I shall not die in this house. I

---

[12] An intimate friend who shared the views of Leo Nikolaevitch, a doctor who lived in the Tolstoys' house from the year 1904. He was of Slovak nationality, and in 1920 left Russia and returned to Czechoslovakia, where he died in 1921.

[13] From one of the diaries and letters of Tolstoy's friends and household of the times.

have made up my mind to go to a strange place where I shall not be known. And perhaps I may come straight to die in your hut.... I want to prepare for death in peace, and here they think of me as worth so many roubles. I shall go away, I shall certainly go away."

Only a final decisive shock was needed. In his same letter to the student he says about going away: "This can and ought only to be done when it is essential, not for the supposed external objects, but for the satisfaction of the inner need of the soul, — when to remain in the old position becomes as morally impossible as it is physically impossible not to cough when one cannot breathe.... And I am near to that position, and every day I get nearer and nearer to it."

But Leo Nikolaevitch still did not go away, and remaining continued to be subjected on an increased scale to the tortures to which he had been subjected since the 'eighties. And he remained still for the same reasons as had restrained him for thirty years. He knew that he would not alleviate the position of the peasants of the district by going. From his painful position in the eyes of men he drew a profitable lesson in humility. His wife's attitude to him assisted in him the development of true love for those who hated his soul. And therefore the more intense these trials became with the passage of time, the more painfully they were reflected in his soul, the more difficult it became for him to deal with them — the more insistent from the spiritual point of view became the moral duty not to forsake his post, but to endure to the end.

CHAPTER III

THE HISTORY OF THE WILL

In order to understand why Sofya Andreyevna's attitude to Leo Nikolaevitch was so exasperated, and what impelled her to treat him so cruelly, it is essential to have some conception why he found it necessary about this time to make a will, leaving all his writings free to the public.

The story of Tolstoy's will is so complicated and full of details that a separate circumstantial account of it is required. Here I will only briefly state the most essential facts.

At the beginning of the 'eighties, at the time when the spiritual regeneration of Leo Nikolaevitch was taking place, though his new attitude of completely disapproving of property was not yet fully defined, he made over to his wife an authorisation for the publication and sale of his collected works, the income from which was the principal source of the material means by which his family lived. Later on, when he came to realise that property of every kind

23

was wrong, he did not, in spite of all his efforts, succeed in persuading Sofya Andreyevna to renounce this income voluntarily and to give him back the authorisation he had given her. He did not feel morally justified in forcibly depriving her of what she clung to so passionately, and what against the will of Leo Nikolaevitch she considered had been put at the disposal of the family for ever. This trading in his works by his wife against his wish was, in his own words, one of the most agonising sufferings of his life. All his new works, however, those that had appeared after 1881 and those destined to appear later, he thereupon freed from the monopoly of his family, announcing in a letter to the newspapers, that all who wished could reprint them without any fee. Sofya Andreyevna had, willy-nilly, to submit to this decision on the part of the author. But every time when, instead of articles of a religious and social character, which did not in the literary market command the immense value enjoyed by his artistic works, Leo Nikolaevitch undertook any work in artistic form, Sofya Andreyevna was so much excited and so persistently demanded that the publication of the new work should be handed over to her for the benefit of the family, that it completely destroyed the spiritual tranquillity which he needed for concentrated creative work.

Many times repeated, these family scenes led him to decide to print no more works of art during his lifetime.[14] And this decision of his

---

[14] This decision, which Leo Nikolaevitch reached alone with his conscience, he tried to keep a secret from everyone, and when, guessing from certain signs how it was, I told him on one occasion, he was much puzzled to know how I could have discovered his secret. To explain why this decision not to publish his artistic work during his lifetime put a stop to Leo Nikolaevitch's work upon them, it must be pointed out that it was his habit to make the chief revision of his first rough sketches on the proofs sent him from the printer's. Besides, if he had merely worked at them in manuscript he would have been subjected to the same persistent

is the real reason why, during the latter period of his life, he gave so little to humanity in that sphere.

In the end Sofya Andreyevna began quite openly to declare, even in the presence of Leo Nikolaevitch, that after his death, according to the advice of lawyers whom she had consulted, his renunciation of all literary property in the works of the second period would lose its validity, and that those works also would, like all the rest, become the property of his family. Besides this she began to insist that Leo Nikolaevitch should give her a fresh authorisation for the sale of his writings of the first period for a long time in the future and also give her the right to prosecute at law anyone who should infringe the copyright.

In his diary for 1909 Leo Nikolaevitch writes: "Last night I felt wretched after talking to Sofya Andreyevna about publishing my works and prosecuting. If she only knew and understood how she alone poisons the last hours, days, months, of my life! I do not know how to say it to her and have no hope that anything one could say would produce the slightest effect upon her."[15]

---

persecution which so distracted his peace and his concentration upon his work. (Sofya Andreyevna told me that she had actually exacted a promise from him not to give anyone but herself his manuscripts to copy.)

[15] D. P. Makovitsky in his diary says the same thing: "In 1909 before the Stockholm Peace Congress, Sofya Andreyevna wanted to prosecute I. I. Gorbunov for publishing The Prisoner in the Caucasus, and sent Torba (a Court official, her helper in publishing Tolstoy's works) to see a lawyer. The lawyer asked what authority Sofya Andreyevna had for instituting proceedings. 'She has a deed of trust for transacting all Leo Nikolaevitch's affairs.' 'This is not enough, she must have a deed transferring the copyright to her.' Sofya Andreyevna asked Leo Nikolaevitch for it, but he refused point blank. Then Sofya Andreyevna had recourse to hysterics and did not let Leo Nikolaevitch go to Stockholm. In the summer of that year she started playing very cleverly the same game (this time against

Becoming convinced that this greed of Sofya Andreyevna on behalf of the family would only increase with years, and that she really was capable of taking possession of all his works after his death and of depriving other publishers of the possibility of printing them, Leo Nikolaevitch felt himself morally bound to guard against such a monopolisation of his writings. And he was so firmly convinced that it was his duty before God and men to do this, that in spite of all that he had to endure on account of it afterwards, he remained unshaken upon this point right up to his death, which was brought about by the spiritual sufferings which were inflicted upon him in consequence of this.[16]

Tchertkoff), pretending to be ill in order to force Leo Nikolaevitch to give her the copyright. It was not Sofya Andreyevna who said the other thing, but Misha and Andryusha. They blurted out about the will."—(Sept. 14, 1910, Kotchety.)

[16] A clear light is thrown upon what Leo Nikolaevitch had to endure in this connection by a letter which a relation of his, the lawyer I. V. Denisenko, wrote for my benefit when I was exiled from the province of Tula in 1909, and being unable to be at Yasnaya Polyana, did not know what was taking place there. I append a few abstracts from the letter to complete the picture:

"In the July of 1909, when I was at Yasnaya Polyana, Leo Nikolaevitch Tolstoy was intending to go to the Peace Congress at Stockholm, and Sofya Andreyevna was opposed to this. This provoked a regular series of misunderstandings and Sofya Andreyevna fell ill, not wishing Leo Nikolaevitch to go to the Congress.

"It happened once that she called me into her bedroom, and showing me a general authorisation for the management of their affairs given her long ago by Leo Nikolaevitch, asked me whether she could upon this authorisation sell to a third person the right of publishing his work, and, what was still more important, institute proceedings against Sergeyenko and some teacher in a military school for making books of extracts and anthologies from the works of Leo Nikolaevitch on the ground that these books of extracts would cause her, Sofya Andreyevna, considerable material damage....

After carefully thinking over all the circumstances of the case and taking advice of persons conversant with the subject, Leo Nikolaevitch came to the conclusion that if he really desired that his writings should be freely accessible to everyone after his death, he could not secure his object without making a formal will. And therefore, with this end in view, he decided to have recourse to that means. The editorship and first publication of all his posthumous works he entrusted to me, with the understanding that everything brought out by me should at once become public property. And in order to make the fulfilment of this task secure in practice, he made a formal will in favour of his younger daughter Alexandra Lvovna, which would make it possible for her to safeguard my task from any attempts to hinder it. The profit on the first issue of his works after his death he assigned in the first place for the redemption of the Yasnaya Polyana estate from the Tolstoy family in order to hand it over to the peasants, and this was duly carried out after his death.

"I believe it was on the day after that that I was in the park picking berries with my wife and children. My wife asked me to go for something to the lodge. I went along an avenue, passing between flower-beds, and there quite unexpectedly I came upon Leo Nikolaevitch. I was struck by his appearance. He was bowed and he looked worried and exhausted. His eyes were dim and he seemed weak as I had never seen him before. He caught hurriedly at my arm on meeting me, and said with tears in his eyes: 'Ivan Vassilyevitch, darling, what is she doing to me? What is she doing to me? She is insisting on having an authorisation for instituting proceedings. You know I can't do that.... It would be against my principles.'

"Then walking a few steps with me he said: 'I have a great favour to ask of you, only let it be a secret between us. For the time don't speak of it to anyone, not even to Sasha. Please make up a deed for me by which I could announce publicly that I give all my works at whatever date they may have been written freely for the benefit of all.'"

Of course the legal form of the will could not but be distasteful to Leo Nikolaevitch. But this was to some extent counterbalanced in his eyes by the fact that the object of the will was not prosecution of anyone in the future, but, on the contrary, the prevention of the possibility of legal proceedings being taken by persons who might put in claims to inherit proprietary rights in the works of Leo Nikolaevitch if there had been no such will.

There was also another disagreeable side to this business for Leo Nikolaevitch. To avoid in connection with the will any altercations and dissensions, which would have been undesirable in themselves and would have made the position of Alexandra Lvovna, as legal heiress of his manuscripts, utterly impossible in the family, Leo Nikolaevitch resolved not to tell anyone of his will. Though to keep the fact of the existence of a will secret is a fairly usual thing to do in such circumstances, it will be readily understood that it was against the grain for Leo Nikolaevitch, and he resolved to act in this way solely because he saw no other alternative.[17]

---

[17] There was even a moment when these two undesirable conditions associated with the will, i.e. its legal form and the secrecy accompanying it, caused Leo Nikolaevitch to feel doubts as to the rectitude of his action. These doubts were aroused by a conversation with one of his intimate friends, who came in from outside and knew little of the circumstances of this complicated affair. Leo Nikolaevitch, who was distinguished by an extreme degree of touching sensitiveness to every criticism of his behaviour, agreed with his friend that he had acted, as the latter asserted, "inconsistently," and he told me of it, declaring, however, that he should nevertheless not change the dispositions he had made. On my side I was compelled to reply that in that case of course I should refuse to be his future executor for carrying out his testamentary dispositions, since only a conviction that I was accomplishing his definite and conscious desire could give me the necessary moral support for the performance of this difficult and responsible duty. At the same time, in accordance with his request, I reminded him of the circumstances and considerations which

had induced him to have recourse to a will. In answer I received from him the following letter:

"I write this on little scraps of paper because I am in the woods out for a walk. Ever since yesterday evening I have been thinking about your yesterday's letter. The two chief feelings which it aroused in me were repulsion for the manifestations of coarse greed and heartlessness which I either did not see or have seen and forgotten, and distress and repentance that I should have hurt you by the letter in which I expressed regret for what I had done. The deduction I have made from the letter is that N. N. was wrong, and also that I was wrong in agreeing with him, and that I fully approve your conduct, but all the same am not satisfied with my own: I feel that it was possible to act better, but I don't know how. Now I do not regret what I have done, i.e. that I have made the will I did make, and I can only be thankful to you for the interest you have taken in the matter.

"I shall tell Tanya about it to-day, and that will be very pleasant to me.

"Leo Tolstoy.

"Aug. 12, 1910."

In his private pocket diary on Aug. 11, 1910, Leo Nikolaevitch wrote as follows:

"A long letter from Tchertkoff describing all that has gone before. Very sad. Painful to read and recall. He is perfectly right, and I feel to blame in regard to him. N. N. was wrong. I will write to both of them."

Certain persons who, for one reason or another, do not sympathise with the testamentary dispositions of Leo Nikolaevitch, and especially those of them who took a personal share in the upsetting of them, continue to this day to assert that Leo Nikolaevitch saw in the end that he had made a mistake and regretted that he had made a will.

In confirmation of this they quote a few words written by Leo Nikolaevitch in his pocket diary at the time of his doubts; but they are carefully silent with regard to the later note in the same diary which I have just quoted.

In reality, of course, this incident of Leo Nikolaevitch's hesitation can only serve to prove how consciously from every point of view he weighed and considered all the circumstances of the case. If no doubts had ever assailed him it would have been possible to admit the supposition that it had never occurred to him to look at the question from the other side, and that therefore his attitude to it was one-sided. But now we know that he not only took a critical attitude as to his action, but that at one time he even

Sofya Andreyevna's fears that Leo Nikolaevitch might make a will depriving his family of the copyright of his works were the underlying cause of her hostile attitude to him. It was on account of this that she made such efforts, on the one hand to wring out of him the complete transfer of all rights in his works to her, and on the other hand by incessant watchfulness over him to eliminate all possibility of his signing any business document without her knowledge. And it was for this same reason that she was filled with such hatred for me personally, assuming, though quite mistakenly, that the initiative in Leo Nikolaevitch's renunciation of his copyrights and the arrangements for carrying this out came from me.

Leo Nikolaevitch was so firm in his resolution to leave his writings for the free use of all, that with his own hand he wrote a will in accordance with that idea, not once only but several times, owing to the fact that the legal form of the documents he composed were never sufficiently correct to secure the required authority for them. The last time he made his will while Sofya Andreyevna was watching over him most vigilantly, during a ride on horseback in the thickest part of the forest, having previously invited three persons of the circle of friends living with me at Telyatniki near Yasnaya Polyana to meet him there and witness his signature.

By making this will Leo Nikolaevitch secured that after his death his writings became accessible to all, and not the property of his family. This result in itself is of vast social importance, seeing that it

---

doubted if it were right. If, even after such hesitation, he yet definitely confirmed his desire that the will should remain in force, what can be a better proof that this his final decision expresses his real and fully conscious will?—Cf. Diary, Vol. I. ed. 1916; Appendix, p. 260, "The Will," July 22, 1910.

gave the working people—the poorest class of all countries—access to Tolstoy's works in the cheapest form, since it was open to any number of publishers to print them, and the competition between them would bring down the price of the books.

But apart from this purely practical gain for the vast masses of mankind, the struggle between Leo Nikolaevitch and his wife for the copyright of his works,—the struggle which cost him his life,— had also a great significance from the ideal side. It displayed before the eyes of mankind, present and future, an extremely important truth in connection with the Christian doctrine of the non-resistance to evil by force which Tolstoy so vividly set forth and lighted up in his writings. Leo Nikolaevitch completely sacrificing himself showed in practice that this principle does not lead, as many suppose, to helplessly giving in to evil and allowing it to triumph unchecked. Unyieldingly maintaining his rejection of copyright in the interests of the working masses of mankind, he confirmed by his example, plain to the whole world, what the less eminent "non-resistants" are continually exemplifying in their life. He showed that people of such a theory of life do not give in to evil, but are continually struggling against it in the best and truest way, by refusing to take part in it. He showed also that to yield to the demand of others from meekness and love for them is only admissible up to the limit beyond which they try to make one do what is against one's conscience; and that when people's demands pass beyond those limits, one ought not to yield to them in any way in spite of any sufferings oneself or those one loves may have to bear.

No insistence on the part of those nearest him, no sufferings of his own on account of it, were able to compel him in this case to depart from what he considered himself bound to do. Is it possible to find a more convincing proof that Tolstoy recognised it as morally necessary to resist evil in the most resolute way? — and it was just in consequence of this resistance to evil that he had to sacrifice both his peace and his life.

In a letter to me of September 10, 1910, Leo Nikolaevitch writes of his inner experience in a way which is highly significant. He says: "Of late, not with my brains but with my sides, as the peasants say, I have come to a clear understanding of the difference between the resistance which is returning evil for evil and the resistance of refusing to yield in the line of conduct which one recognises as one's duty to one's conscience and God. I will try."

At the same time by his attitude to the very idea of literary property Tolstoy, by the exceptional sincerity and consistency of his manner of action, has helped and still more will help his literary brethren to see clearly in this "delicate" question, to shut their eyes to which has now become impossible. As time passes a greater and greater number of writers will undoubtedly be troubled by doubts as to whether it is not as morally reprehensible to traffic in one's words, in one's soul, as to traffic in one's body, and Tolstoy's attitude will serve conscientious writers as a guiding star in illuminating this question.

One cannot but recognise Tolstoy's conspicuous services in all this. And though he acted as he did without considering what bearing this would have on the consciousness of men, merely striving not to let himself be drawn into an action contrary to his conscience, nevertheless this first renunciation of literary property on the part of one of the greatest writers of the world undoubtedly has a vast significance for humanity.

If in my present brief account of Tolstoy's leaving home I have had to dwell rather minutely upon the question of his will, it is because all the threads of the complicated conditions and circumstances which caused his departure meet about that central question. It is true that some of those near to Leo Nikolaevitch have tried to persuade themselves that Sofya Andreyevna's attitude to him, which made it impossible for him to remain longer with her, was chiefly provoked by property interests not connected with his will. They ascribe her conduct to various causes and principally to her neurotic condition and morbid, abnormal jealousy. Although putting the matter in such a light is undoubtedly due to affectionate goodwill to Sofya Andreyevna, I consider it my duty to protest against such an interpretation most decisively in the interests of truth, which here as everywhere is more important than anything. We ought not to hide from ourselves that there are more than a sufficient quantity of facts going to prove that Sofya Andreyevna in this case acted first of all, and most of all, under the influence of feelings and considerations immediately concerned with the material prosperity of her numerous family, consisting, as she was continually reminding people, of twenty-eight persons, counting children and grandchildren. It is essential to keep this circumstance in view in order to have a correct understanding of the attitude of Leo Nikolaevitch to his will.

True love for people dead and alive alike is not shown by concealing their mistakes and failures from oneself and others, but in knowing how, in spite of all the undesirable qualities which every one of us has in sufficient quantity, to behave to one another with compassion and tolerance, recognising that everyone is responsible for all. Then we shall not try to pass by the weak spots without noticing them, or to smear over the cracks on the outside, but shall, on the contrary, display them in order that they may be corrected by the efforts of all.

The above-mentioned circumstances and motives of the testamentary dispositions of Leo Nikolaevitch in regard to his writings must be kept in mind if one is to have a true conception of his position in the family at the period immediately preceding his "going away." An acquaintance with those circumstances and impulses makes it possible to understand the true character of the relations which have been formed between Leo Nikolaevitch and her with whom he had been connected for forty-eight long years and out of love and pity for whom he was ready to sacrifice all but his conscience.

CHAPTER IV

INTERVALS OF REST—IN OTHER PEOPLE'S HOUSES

The only intervals of freedom and rest which Leo Nikolaevitch could enjoy from the indescribably painful conditions of life at Yasnaya Polyana at that period were afforded him by the rare occasions when he succeeded in getting away for a week or two to stay with some one of his more intimate friends. Thus during the last year of his life he stayed on two occasions with his daughter Tatyana Lvovna, in the Mtsensk district, and with me (I was in exile from the Tula province), the first time at Kryokshino in the Zvenigorodsky district near Moscow, and afterwards at Meshtcherskoe in the Serpuhovsky district. But he very rarely succeeded in arranging these visits, and only did so with great trouble, since Sofya Andreyevna opposed them in every way; and if, in spite of her opposition, he did make up his mind to go away, it would sometimes happen that at the last minute she would decide

35

to go with him, which, of course, spoilt the chief object of the excursion.

I remember on both occasions when he came to us how extremely shattered, worn out and ill Leo Nikolaevitch looked, and how perceptibly before our eyes he improved physically and revived spiritually. Even on the second or third day of a calm life, and in a circle of friends of the same way of thinking, who guarded his spiritual peace and fully respected his independence, he was completely changed. It was as though some crushing, agonising burden had fallen off him; his face was brighter in expression, his movements became vigorous, in the morning he worked with concentration for many hours on end at his writings, amazing us all by the number of written pages which he afterwards gave us to copy out. During his daily walks he went so rapidly and so far that it was difficult for people much younger to keep up with him. With the visitors of the most varied kind, of whom numbers were always flocking to see him, and from whom no one in our house shut him off as at home, he carried on lively conversations in his free time, in that way coming into direct contact with the surrounding world. In conversation with his friends no one interrupted him or contradicted him at every turn, an annoyance to which he was continually subjected at home, and therefore communion with those surrounding him here afforded him joyous spiritual relief. Everything showed what vast stores of energy were still preserved in him; it was clear that under favourable conditions he might for many years to come lead an active life to the joy and profit of humanity.

His inner spiritual revival was shown very conspicuously in the fact that every day he became more and more drawn to artistic creation. At first he noted down characteristic meetings and conversations which took place during his walks. And each time before he went away he told me with confident eagerness that great, purely artistic works were stirring within him and taking shape in his soul, and that he hoped now to set to work upon them. But these plans were not destined to be realised, since on his return to Yasnaya Polyana the painful conditions which have been indicated already were renewed, and calm creative work was inconsistent with them.

Altogether the difference between his condition, both physical and spiritual, when he arrived and when he left us was striking. I remember how I met him in the garden at the end of his last stay with us at Meshtcherskoe, where he had arrived almost in a state of collapse. He walked quickly and he looked remarkably vigorous and many years younger. With an air of lively surprise he greeted me with the words: "I don't understand what it is in your diet, but whenever I stay with you my digestion seems to become perfect." It is well known that the best conditions for a man suffering from defective digestion are simple, not elaborately prepared, food adapted to his requirements, and above all an even, untroubled spiritual atmosphere in all his home life. But Leo Nikolaevitch expected so little by way of attention from others to his needs and tastes, he attached so little significance for himself to the influence of external surroundings, that it seemed as though it did not enter his head to connect the state of his health with the conditions surrounding him.

CHAPTER V

THE LAST PERIOD

The last and most painful period of Leo Nikolaevitch's life at Yasnaya Polyana began in June 1910, when, on a visit at my summer bungalow at Meshtcherskoe, in the province of Moscow, he was suddenly summoned back to Yasnaya Polyana by a telegram from Sofya Andreyevna, informing him of her sudden illness; as it afterwards turned out, a sham one.

On his return to Yasnaya Polyana, Sofya Andreyevna surrounded his life with new restrictions, finally depriving him of even the limited share of personal freedom which he had until that time enjoyed. She gave up respecting his hours of literary work, for which she had once shown consideration, and by continually bursting in upon him and making scenes, she made it impossible for him to devote himself to the literary work in which he recognised his service to men. His daily walks had become his sole recreation and solace, and now she began to hinder him from going where he wished to go, and from taking with him those whom he wanted to take. She insisted that he should completely give up seeing those of his most intimate friends whose supposed influence on him she feared.[18] Even inside the house she subjected all his actions and conversations to a control which was never relaxed, not disdaining even the most indelicate methods, as, for instance, eavesdropping, with her shoes off at doors, and altogether watching day and night over every action he took. As has already been mentioned, she was demanding from him such an authorisation for the disposal of his works as would give her the power to take legal proceedings in connection with them, and to retain the copyright over a prolonged period in the future. Apprehensive of what he might write in his diary, she tried to prevent his giving the manuscript books of his diary to anyone whatever, even to those whom he charged with work of one sort or another in connection with them, or in whose keeping he desired

---

[18] The members of Tolstoy's household who were most intimate with him—Alexandra Lvovna Tolstoy, D. P. Makovitsky and Varvara Mihailovna Feokritova—were convinced that Sofya Andreyevna's hatred of me was a sham. This is proved, for instance, by the following extract from Makovitsky's diary:

"While I was riding with Leo Nikolaevitch to-day, I was thinking of Sofya Andreyevna's behaviour since June 24, and I came to the conclusion that in reality she is not, and never has been, jealous of Tchertkoff. She pretended to be jealous simply in order to separate him from Leo Nikolaevitch, and prevent him from influencing Leo Nikolaevitch; she thought it was due to Tchertkoff's influence that Leo Nikolaevitch wanted to give away his works to the public....

"And how well she played the part and deceived L. N., Tchertkoff, Tatyana Lvovna, and me (we were all convinced that she was jealous of Tchertkoff). I spoke of this to-day, and Varvara Mihailovna and Alexandra Lvovna answered that they had noticed the same thing long ago (that is, that there was no jealousy), and had put it down in their diaries" (October 13, 1910).

them to be preserved for the sake of greater security. She secretly stole from his pockets those very private diaries which he kept and carried about with him during the most painful periods of his life and scrupulously preserved from every human eye. Not only did she fail to conceal from him and others her distrust and—terrible to say—hatred for him, but openly in the hearing of all gave utterance to these feelings and often expressed them to him in so harsh a form that it brought on heart attacks and even fainting fits in him. She was jealous, or pretended to be jealous, of some of his most intimate friends, bound to him by the closest spiritual unity. In this connection also she openly expressed to those about her, and to outsiders and to Leo Nikolaevitch himself, such incredibly revolting suspicions as the tongue cannot bring itself to repeat, thereby reducing Leo Nikolaevitch almost to complete collapse and driving him to lock all the doors of his room. And with all this she did everything she could to prevent his going away from Yasnaya Polyana, even for the briefest visits which might have enabled him to have at least some rest from the atmosphere of his home, and to gain fresh strength to endure further tortures.

All these requests and others similar to them Sofya Andreyevna did not merely put in words before Leo Nikolaevitch, but if he refused, tried by her whole behaviour to force him against his will to submit to her.[19] For this purpose she resorted to simulated fits of hysteria

---

[19] D. P. Makovitsky records the following incident:
"The day before yesterday she made a scene again: fell at Leo Nikolaevitch's feet and begged him to give her the keys of the safe in the bank where his diaries or the will were kept. Leo Nikolaevitch said that he could not do it and went out. As he passed under her windows Sofya Andreyevna leaned out and cried, 'I have taken opium.' Leo Nikolaevitch rushed upstairs to her, but she met him with the words, 'That was not true, I did not take any.' This scene upset Leo Nikolaevitch very much, and he said to Sofya Andreyevna, 'You are doing all you can to make me leave

and madness, threatened to commit suicide, pretended that she would swallow or had swallowed poison, ran half dressed out of doors in the rain or snow or at night, making them search for her all over the park, and running in to him at any time of the day or the night, even when, utterly exhausted, he had dropped asleep, and waking him up with the object of worrying the concessions she wanted out of him. There is no recounting all the unutterably cruel means to which she unhesitatingly resorted for the sake of forcibly compelling him. And when the members of her family told her that she would kill him by such conduct, she answered coldly that his soul had long been dead for her and that she did not care for his body; and if she were asked what she would do and how she would feel if he really did die of her treatment, she would say, "I shall go at last to Italy; I have never been there."

Leo Nikolaevitch for his part, so long as he thought it right to remain with his wife, tried with strikingly touching meekness to gratify all her wishes and to comply with all her demands which did not run counter to his conscience. When he considered them unreasonable, at first he refused, but as she obstinately insisted and resorted to her usual methods, in the end he often gave way in those cases also; at one time regarding her as quite insane, and being apprehensive that in a moment of frenzy she really might do herself some mischief.

He was only unhesitating in his resistance when his conscience told him that he ought not to give way. Thus, in spite of all Sofya Andreyevna's importunities and strategy, he made his will and did not change it to the end; he did not give her the authority to take

---

home.' After this he had palpitations and almost fainted. He had attempted to run up the stairs, and during those moments of terror and agitation was living through his wife's death" (July 19, 1910)

legal proceedings; he did not hand over his diaries to her, but put them in a place of safety (in the bank at Tula). But since what was most necessary for her object was just that in which he found it impossible to give way to her, it was precisely with these demands that she persecuted him most. And so all his concessions, instead of pacifying her, only encouraged her in more persistent importunities and still more cruel means of oppression.

CHAPTER VI

MENTAL AGONY

It will be readily understood that no health could hold out against such torments lasting over several months at a stretch, no less severe, it may be said, than the tortures of the Inquisition, and exceeding them in their uninterrupted persistence and prolongation. And indeed, returning to Yasnaya in a vigorous and excellent state of health, Leo Nikolaevitch began visibly fading away before her eyes in the nightmare period of the last months of his life: in the course of a few weeks he looked so old and drawn, so weak and thin, so pale and in every respect so physically run down as to be unrecognisable. In the course of those months he had several attacks of faintness. By the day of his departure he looked only the shadow of himself: his heart, his nerves, all his forces were utterly undermined, and of course, under such conditions, the slightest ailment was sure to carry him off, as happened indeed with the first cold he chanced to catch immediately after he went away.

All Sofya Andreyevna's conduct during those last months of their life together revealed to Leo Nikolaevitch much in her that he had never noticed before. He was not only led to doubt of his cherished dream of softening her heart by his all-forgiving love; he began even to feel uncertain whether he were doing her harm or good by being near her, and whether the doctors were not right who in her interests advised them to live apart.[20] And in the end he became convinced that his presence really was a direct incitement to evil for her, calling out and accentuating all the worst sides of her character. Speaking of his departure with that same Novikov a week before it took place, Leo Nikolaevitch said: "For my own sake I have not done this and could not do it, but now I see that it would be better for my family, there would be less dispute among them on my account, less sin."

Another reason that had previously restrained him from going away lay in the fact that he considered that the ordeal to which he was continually exposed in his wife's company was profitable for his own soul, and found in it a spiritual satisfaction. But in the end

---

[20] At the advice of all his friends and members of his household Leo Nikolaevitch went in September to stay with his daughter Tatyana Lvovna Suhotin (at Kotchety) in order to have a rest from family scenes. But Sofya Andreyevna would not leave him in peace even there. This is what we read in Makovitsky's diary:
"This is the third day that Sofya Andreyevna is perfectly frantic. Leo Nikolaevitch sent me to her several times during the day; in the morning she was in her room; she complained of headache and said that she had taken no food for two days; in the afternoon she ran off into the garden.
"Sofya Andreyevna spent the whole day by herself in the park. Leo Nikolaevitch sent me to find her.
"'Oh, Dushan Petrovitch!' he said to me, 'it's worse than ever; everything is going to the worst. Sofya Andreyevna insists that I should go away with her. But I simply cannot do it, for her demands go crescendo and crescendo. I don't know what to do!'" (September 11, 1910, Kotchety.)

Sofya Andreyevna, as she herself expressed it after his death, "overdid it" in her behaviour with him, putting him in such a position that instead of satisfaction he began to experience the sense of awkwardness and shame which one feels in taking part in something unbecoming, unseemly. Two days before he went away he wrote to me: "I feel something unbefitting, something shameful in my position." And in the letter to Alexandra Lvovna the day after he went away he says: "I do not feel that shame, that awkwardness, that lack of freedom which I always used to feel at home." In his last letter to Sofya Andreyevna from Shamardino he states even more definitely that to return to her when she is in such a state of mind would be equivalent to committing suicide, and he did not consider that he had a right to do that. So by now he no longer believed that staying with Sofya Andreyevna was profitable for his own soul, and recognised it as undesirable.

In the course of the later years his hesitation had increased with every day, and at times he seemed to be on the very point of flight.[21] He only stayed through not feeling as yet that irresistible impulse which, as he so well recognised, was essential in order that he might take this momentous step, not through rational considerations alone, but with all his soul, confidently and inevitably. And so long as this impulse was lacking and he was more or less weighing the pros and cons of his departure, the

---

[21] Thus in D. P. Makovitsky's diary we read:
"Leo Nikolaevitch spoke to Alexandra Lvovna of how heavy their family atmosphere was, and said that if it had not been for her he would have gone away. He is on the alert. Yesterday morning he asked me what were the morning trains to the south. He had said to Marya Alexandrovna, and before that to us, that he has not been able to work for the last four months and that Sofya Andreyevna keeps running in to him, and always suspecting that some secrets are being concealed from her, written documents and conversations" (October 26, 1910).

consideration that for him personally to go away would be a relief, and that there would be more self-sacrifice in remaining, retained its force. Thus I have been told that two days before his departure, when he informed his old friend, the old lady Marya Alexandrovna Schmidt (who, by the way, later on fully understood and approved his departure), that he thought of leaving Yasnaya Polyana, and she thereupon exclaimed: "Leo Nikolaevitch darling, it will pass, it is a moment's weakness," he hastened to reply: "Yes, yes, I know that it is a weakness and I hope that it will pass."

So that in spite of the fact that Leo Nikolaevitch had now become aware of a new phase in Sofya Andreyevna's relations to him, which in reality removed any reasonable purpose in his remaining at her side, and justified his departure, since his presence was becoming bad for her and unprofitable for him, nevertheless he still lingered on, dreading to act prematurely, and as it were waiting for the last decisive shock.

And this shock was not long in coming with startling abruptness.

CHAPTER VII

THE NIGHT OF TOLSTOY'S GOING AWAY

It happened very simply. On the night of the 27th October, at a time when it was supposed that Leo Nikolaevitch was asleep, as he lay in bed he heard and saw through a crack in his door Sofya Andreyevna steal softly into his study and search among the papers on his writing-table. Then as she was going away, noticing the light in his room, she went in and began with an anxious face inquiring how he was. This cold hypocrisy on her part apparently destroyed the last illusion of Leo Nikolaevitch. Only a few days before he had been touched by the solicitude with which Sofya Andreyevna, coming into his bedroom in the same way at night, had climbed on to a chair and had set right the movable frame which had been insecurely fastened. Now he remembered that he had heard a rustle the night before too, and the real value of Sofya Andreyevna's care of him was suddenly revealed to him. Chance had unmasked the awful, systematic comedy which was being played from day to day

47

around him, and in which he had unconsciously to play the central part.

In his diary he describes what he endured that night as follows: —

"I went to bed at half-past eleven, slept till three o'clock. Woke again. As on previous nights, the opening of doors and footsteps. On the previous nights I did not look towards my door; this time I glanced towards it and saw through the crack a bright light in the study and heard rustling. It was Sofya Andreyevna looking for something, probably reading something. On the evening before she begged and insisted that I should not lock the doors. Both her doors were opened so that she could hear my slightest movement. Both by day and by night all my movements and my words must be known to her and be under her control. Again footsteps, a cautious opening of the door and she goes out. I don't know why that aroused in me an irrepressible repulsion and indignation. I tried to go to sleep. I could not; I turned from side to side for about an hour, lighted a candle and sat up. The door opens and Sofya Andreyevna walks in, asking after my health and wondering at the light which she has seen in my room. Repulsion and indignation grow. I am breathless; I count my pulse seventy-seven. I cannot lie still, and suddenly take a final resolution to go away. I write her a letter; I begin packing what is most necessary, only to get away. I wake Dushan, then Sasha; they help me to pack."

As Alexandra Lvovna described, she and her companion Varvara Mihailovna (the amanuensis) were awake that night. She kept fancying that someone was walking about and talking overhead. She was afraid that discussions were taking place between her father and mother. They fell asleep towards morning, but soon heard a knock at the door. Alexandra Lvovna went to the door and opened it.

"Who is it?" she asked.

"It is I, Leo Nikolaevitch.... I am going away at once ... for good.... Come and help me pack."

Alexandra Lvovna said afterwards that she would never forget his figure in the doorway, in a blouse, with a candle in his hand and a bright face resolute and beautiful.

In haste to get away, Leo Nikolaevitch dreaded one thing only: that Sofya Andreyevna might come upon him before he succeeded in getting off, and the calm realisation of his unalterable decision might thereby be troubled.

"I tremble at the thought that she will hear, will come out—a scene, hysterics, and no getting away in the future without a scene. By six o'clock everything has been packed after a fashion. I go to the stable to order the horses; Sasha and Varya finish the packing.... It is night, pitch dark. I get off the path to the lodge, fall into the bushes, get scratched, knock against trees, fall down, lose my cap, cannot find it; with difficulty make my way out, go home, take a cap, and with a lantern make my way to the stable and order the horses to be harnessed. Sasha, Dushan, Varya come. I tremble, expecting pursuit. But at last we get off. At Shtchekino we wait an hour, and every minute I expect her to appear. But at last we are in the railway carriage and set off. Alarm passes, and pity for her rises, but no doubt as to whether I have done what I ought. Perhaps I am mistaken in justifying myself but it seems to me that I have saved myself not as Leo Nikolaevitch, but have saved what at times at least to some small degree there is in me."

49

CHAPTER VIII

TOLSTOY'S RELATION TO HIS WIFE

After his departure Leo Nikolaevitch never for a minute repented what he had done, and never considered the idea of his return to Sofya Andreyevna. When his daughter Alexandra Lvovna several days afterwards asked him whether he could regret his action, he answered: "Of course not. Can a man regret something when he could not act differently?"

And why he could not act differently he told her openly in his letter of the 29th October: "For me, with this spying, eavesdropping, everlasting reproaches, disposing of me according to caprice, everlasting control, pretence of hatred for the man who is nearest and most necessary to me, with this obvious hatred for me and affectation of love ... such a life is not merely unpleasant for me, but utterly impossible. If anyone is to drown oneself it is not she but I....
I desire one thing only, freedom from her, from the falsity, hypocrisy and malice with which her whole being is saturated....

50

All her behaviour to me not only shows a lack of love, but seems to have been unmistakably aimed at killing me...."

These words broke from Leo Nikolaevitch like the irrepressible shriek from the tortured soul of a man who had for long years been accustomed to hide in himself the deepest and most poignant of his sufferings. And therefore after giving vent for once to his need to speak out to his favourite daughter, he at once hastens to comment: "You see, dear, how bad I am. I do not conceal myself from you."[22]

This letter is important for us, Leo Nikolaevitch's friends, because it raises a little corner of the curtain with which for the last ten years of his life he scrupulously covered from the eye of man the inner tortures he experienced. Were it not for this "human document" it might have been supposed that, having attained the marvellous height of spiritual illumination which distinguished the latter period of his life, Leo Nikolaevitch was thereby saved from the possibility of feeling insult and experiencing spiritual pain. Now we know that if in his diary, in his correspondence and in conversation with his friends he abstained for the most part from any complaints of the bitterness of his position, preferring to note his own mistakes and weaknesses, he did this not because he was at that time free from the common human characteristic of feeling pain inflicted upon him. We now see that to the very end of his days he had not ceased to be for us ordinary people a comrade capable of feeling the same mortifications and sufferings as we. For that reason we ought to be grateful to fate which for one instant revealed before us in that letter the deep spiritual wound which Leo

---

[22] I permit myself to quote this letter without asking Alexandra Lvovna's permission to do so, because it has already, without our previous knowledge, appeared in print in the historical journal, Facts and Days (Petrograd, 1920), and because it makes a less one-sided impression in connection with the other contents of the present book.

Nikolaevitch bore away with him when he left his wife. But at the same time it would be quite a mistake to suppose that though he left Sofya Andreyevna he retained any evil feeling towards her and was not capable of forgiving her. On the contrary, almost at the same time as the letter to his daughter which we have quoted, he wrote his wife a touching, warm-hearted letter which leaves not the slightest doubt of his real love for her. And on the following day he wrote to his two elder children: "Please try and soothe your mother, for whom I have the most sincere feeling of compassion and love." And he not only pitied Sofya Andreyevna, but had so much real love for her that he could with a pure heart forgive her, and himself beg her forgiveness.

Altogether the last letters of Leo Nikolaevitch to his wife, which have, by the way, been published by her,[23] strikingly reveal some characteristic peculiarities in his relations with her during the latest period of their life together. The most conspicuous peculiarity is that in spite of the very painful crises Leo Nikolaevitch had passed through in his family relations, the habitual and extremely delicate consideration in his behaviour to Sofya Andreyevna never left him for one minute. Consequently when telling her the causes of his departure, he does not without necessity touch upon those of his impulses which were disagreeable to her. Avoiding them as far as possible, he accentuates those of his motives which had a general character and did not wound her vanity. He only alludes to the points in which she had been to blame towards him when it is quite unavoidable, and touches on those questions as gently and carefully as possible.

I will quote those of his letters which directly concern his departure, beginning with one written thirteen years before he actually went

---

[23] "Letters of Count L. N. Tolstoy to his wife, 1862-1910" (Kushnerev & Co., 1915).

away, at a time when he was intending to leave his family but did not do so. He directed that this letter should be given to his wife after his death, which was done.

I

"June 8, 1897
"Dear Sonya,

"For a long time past I have been worried by the inconsistency of my life with my convictions. To make you change your life, your habits in which I have trained you, I could not; go away from you hitherto I could not either, thinking that I should deprive the children while they were small of at least that little influence I might have on them, and should be grieving you; nor can I any longer continue to live as I have lived these sixteen years, at one time struggling and irritating you, at another myself, succumbing to the temptations to which I am accustomed, and by which I am surrounded; and I have determined now to do what I have long wanted to do—go away: in the first place, because for me with my advancing years this life becomes more and more oppressive, and I long more and more for solitude; and secondly, because my children are grown up, my influence is not now needed in the house, and all of you have interests more vital to you which will make you feel my absence less.

"The chief thing is that just as the Hindus when close on sixty go away into the forest, as every religious old man longs to devote the last years of his life to God, and not to jests, to puns, to gossip and to tennis, so I, entering on my seventieth year, long with my whole soul for peace, for solitude, and if not for complete harmony, at least not the glaring discord between one's life and one's convictions, one's conscience.

"If I were to do this openly there would be entreaties, upbraidings, arguments, complaints; I should lose courage, perhaps, and not

54

carry out my decision although it ought to be carried out. And therefore please forgive if my action hurts you, and in thy soul do thou, Sonya, especially, let me go with a good will; do not look for me, don't lament over me, or complain against me; do not blame me.

"That I have gone away from you does not show that I was displeased with you. I know that you literally could not see and feel as I do, and therefore could not and cannot change your life and make sacrifices for what you do not recognise. And therefore I do not blame you, but, on the contrary, with love and gratitude remember the thirty-five long years of our life, especially the first half of the time, when with a motherly self-sacrifice, which is part of your nature, you so vigorously and firmly bore that which you considered your vocation. You have given me and the world what you could give—you have given a great deal of motherly love and self-sacrifice, and one cannot but value you for it. But in the later period of our life—the last fifteen years—we have grown apart. I cannot think that I am to blame, because I know that I have changed neither for my own sake nor for other people's, but because I could do nothing else. I cannot blame you either for not following me, but I thank you and think of you, and always shall think of you, with love for what you have given me.

> "Farewell, dear Sonya,
> "Your loving
> "Leo Tolstoy."

(Cf. Letters to his Wife, p. 524.)

II

"My going away will grieve you. I am sorry for it, but do understand and believe that I cannot act differently. My position in the house is becoming, has become, unbearable. Apart from everything else, I cannot any longer live in the conditions of luxury in which I have been living, and I am doing what old men of my age commonly do—they retire from worldly life to spend their last days in solitude and quiet. Please understand this and do not come after me if you find out where I am. Your coming in that way would only make your and my position worse and would not alter my decision.

"I thank you for these forty-eight years of faithful life with me, and beg you to forgive me for anything in which I have been to blame towards you, even as I with all my soul forgive you for anything in which you may have been to blame towards me. I advise you to resign yourself to the new position in which my departure places you, and not to have any ill-feeling against me.

"If you want to communicate with me, give everything to Sasha. She will know where I am and will forward anything that is necessary; she cannot tell you where I am, because I have made her promise not to tell anyone."

(Letters to his Wife, p. 590.)

III

"A meeting between us and still more my return is now utterly impossible. For you it would be, as everyone declares, highly injurious, and for me it would be awful, since now, in consequence of your excitement, irritation and morbid condition, my position would, if that is possible, be worse than ever. I advise you to resign yourself to what has happened, to settle down in your new position, and above all to attend to your health. To say nothing of loving, if you don't absolutely hate me you ought to enter a little into my position. And if you do that you not only will not blame me, but will try to help me to find peace and the possibility of some sort of human life, to help me by controlling yourself, and you will not wish me to come back now. Your mood as at present, your desire to commit suicide and efforts to do so, show more than anything your loss of self-control, and make my return unthinkable at present. No one but yourself can save all who are near you, me and above all yourself, from sufferings such as we have endured in the past.[24]

"Try to direct all your energies not to bringing about what you desire—at present my return—but to bringing peace to your soul, and you will get what you desire.

"I have spent two days at Shamordino and Optina Pustyn, and am

---

[24] The words "sufferings such as we have endured in the past" have been left out of Tolstoy's letters by Sofya Andreyevna without any indication of an omission.

57

going away. I will post this letter on the way. I do not say where I am going, because I consider separation essential both for you and for me. Do not think that I am going away because I do not love you: I love and pity you with all my soul, but I cannot do otherwise than I am doing.

"Your letter I know was written sincerely, but you are not capable of doing what you would wish to. And what matters is not the fulfilment of any of my desires or demands, but only your balance, your calm, reasonable attitude to life. And while that is lacking my life with you is not thinkable. To return to you while you are in such a state would be equivalent to committing suicide. And I do not consider that I have a right to do that. Farewell, dear Sonya. God help you. Life is no jesting matter, and we have no right to throw it away at our own will, and it is unreasonable, too, to measure it by length of time. Perhaps those months which we have left to live are more important than all the years lived before, and we must live them well."

And from the touching interest which Leo Nikolaevitch displayed after he went away in everything relating to Sofya Andreyevna, questioning everyone about her with the greatest emotion and solicitude, it was perfectly clear that, though he recognised before his conscience that to live together with her any longer was impossible, yet in his soul he was fully reconciled with her.

CHAPTER IX

THE MOTIVES THAT DECIDED HIS GOING AWAY

For us, the nearest friends of Leo Nikolaevitch, who watched step by step what was taking place at Yasnaya Polyana during the last days of his presence there, the reason why he could do nothing but go away was easy to understand. But the reader who is not so closely acquainted with all the circumstances may ask, Why exactly did Sofya Andreyevna's behaviour on the last night have such an influence on Leo Nikolaevitch? What did she do then that was new and not to be expected from her previous behaviour?

Of course Sofya Andreyevna's behaviour on that night only gave the final impetus to Leo Nikolaevitch's going away. In reality the question of leaving home had already been decided in his soul, and, as it seems to me, he was, as it were, instinctively only awaiting the inevitable final impulse for carrying out his intention. And the key to the understanding of Leo Nikolaevitch's spiritual state at the time is hidden in the words with which he concluded the note in his diary concerning his departure: "I feel that I have saved myself, not as Leo Nikolaevitch, but have saved what at times at least to some small degree there is in me." These words are marvellous in their touching humility on the lips of a man whose soul was filled to overflowing and was the reflection of the highest principle, and at the same time remarkable from the light which they throw on the deeper motives of his departure. In these words one is conscious of the dread—under the conditions beginning to exist about him—of being deprived of the spiritual independence essential for the preservation of the inviolability of his "holy of holies"—the dread of being deprived of the possibility of resisting the ever-persisting attacks from outside—which might very naturally come to pass, considering Leo Nikolaevitch's extreme age and the gradual weakening of his physical powers.

It must not be forgotten also that by this time he had become convinced of the complete uselessness, even undesirability, of his remaining longer with Sofya Andreyevna, and that therefore the various impulses to go away which he had before so scrupulously repressed in his soul were now set free. The painful consciousness of luxury and privilege in which his life was spent in the midst of the poverty around him, the yearning for peace and solitude before death, and many other causes began without hindrance to impel him in the same direction.

Thus the cup was already full and only the last drop was lacking. And just at this time suddenly the new element in his wife's behaviour which provided that last impulse to departure was revealed to Leo Nikolaevitch.

What was new to him was the sudden revelation of the atmosphere of lying and hypocrisy in which he saw himself entangled. He unexpectedly became the involuntary witness of how Sofya Andreyevna, when she thought he was asleep, secretly stole up to his papers, and of how, as soon as she found out that he was not asleep, she began again at once as though nothing were the matter, expressing solicitude for his health. His eyes were at once opened and he saw what had long been well known to his intimate friends, but what the remnant of confidence in and respect for his wife which were still preserved in his soul, forbade him even to admit in his thoughts: that is, that she was acting a farce with him.

Together with this discovery everything was transformed for Leo Nikolaevitch, and indeed that was inevitable. It was of little moment that the incident which opened his eyes may seem in itself not to be of much importance. For married people who have lived together fifty years the first incident which reveals hypocrisy in one of them is always of importance. This incident at once threw quite a new light for Leo Nikolaevitch on all that had passed between him and Sofya Andreyevna. Till that time he had supposed that he had to do with sincere egoism and ill-will, with open wilfulness and innate coarseness and with morbid abnormality. And meeting this with unvarying mildness, patience and love, he recognised that he was doing as he ought, and therefore felt an inner satisfaction. Now all this was turned upside down. In the past the position had been clear; before him was a definite evil which laid on him as definite a duty to meet the evil with good. Now he had to do with a sort of tangle in which there was so much falsity that it was impossible to make out where reality ended and deception began; so that instead of his former satisfaction Leo Nikolaevitch suddenly felt the ambiguous position in which he found himself. So at least I explain to myself the extreme emotion which Leo Nikolaevitch felt at his final decision to go away.

It is true that even before this he knew of Sofya Andreyevna's insincere behaviour. A month before he went away he wrote of Sofya Andreyevna in this diary: "I cannot get accustomed to regarding her words as the ravings of delirium. All my trouble comes from that. It is impossible to talk to her, because she does not recognise the obligation of truth nor of logic, nor of her own words, nor of conscience. It is awful. I am not speaking now of love for me, of which there is no trace. She does not want my love for her either; all she wants is that people should think that I love her, and that is so awful." (Diary, September 10, 1910.) Yet apparently Leo Nikolaevitch still had no idea of the degree of insincerity and deception of which Sofya Andreyevna was capable in her relations with him personally. But on that night he was involuntarily brought face to face with the manifestation of it, and he was the more revolted because he had hitherto so scrupulously striven in his soul to preserve some sort of trust in his wife.

Finally, convinced that he was incapable of changing the spiritual condition of Sofya Andreyevna, he saw now that his presence at her side could only serve as a cause of offence for her, exciting the worst side of her nature. And so the former obstacles to his departure were removed from him, and his soul demanded release from the unbefitting position in which he found himself.

It is easy to understand that under such conditions the first serious occasion was sufficient to impel him to carry out his long-cherished intention, and he went away.[25]

---

[25] I have heard—it is true, from very few persons, and those chiefly belonging to Leo Nikolaevitch's family—regret expressed that he did not die peaceably at Yasnaya Polyana in the midst of his family. The picture imagined by these people of the death-bed of Leo Nikolaevitch in the

home of his ancestors, surrounded by all his family, and giving his blessing to his grief-stricken wife, may perhaps be very touching. But such a scene would in reality be impossible, since Sofya Andreyevna was in such a condition of mind that, apart from a simulated exaggeration of feeling and the basest preoccupation with the material heritage, nothing more would have happened than on previous occasions when Leo Nikolaevitch was taken with the attacks and fainting fits to which he was liable, and it would have been painful for him. We ought, on the contrary, to rejoice that circumstances gave Leo Nikolaevitch the chance of spending the last days of his life and the last hours of his consciousness in a quiet, genuine atmosphere, among intimate friends who truly loved and understood him, and who strenuously watched over his spiritual peace and did not pester him in those last minutes with any worldly cares or material considerations. In this I cannot but see an immense happiness and blessing for Leo Nikolaevitch.

Some people lay stress on the spiritual pain which Sofya Andreyevna must have experienced when she learned that Leo Nikolaevitch had left her. There is no doubt that this pain must have been very severe, particularly at first. But one must not blame others for the sufferings which are the work of the sufferer himself. If my own negligence is the cause of a man slipping off the roof and falling on my head I cannot blame him for the bruises he has caused me by his fall. It is as unjust to blame Leo Nikolaevitch for the suffering caused to Sofya Andreyevna by his departure, which was provoked by herself. Moreover, sufferings which are the result of our own mistakes are often beneficial. So in this instance, if Sofya Andreyevna, toward the end of the life of Leo Nikolaevitch, ever displayed the faintest gleams of consciousness of the great wrong she had done him, it was only at the time of her heaviest suffering on account of his leaving her. And therefore one may regret the causes which called forth Leo Nikolaevitch's departure, but not that the emotional shock given Sofya Andreyevna by it opened her eyes, if only for a few instants, to the true significance of her behaviour to her husband.

If it should seem strange to anyone that Leo Nikolaevitch, even after he had left home, so dreaded an interview with Sofya Andreyevna, that is only because the mental condition in which, as Leo Nikolaevitch well knew, she was at that time is too little known. When he left Yasnaya Polyana Leo Nikolaevitch firmly and unhesitatingly decided to cut himself off from his family, and therefore while he was still hoping to live independently, he naturally avoided interviews with Sofya Andreyevna, who would with all her energies, and without scruple as to the means employed, have hindered his realising his plan. When he was laid up at Astapavo and foresaw the possibility of death being at hand, it was just as natural that he should have felt the need of that spiritual tranquillity to which every dying man has a right. And that Sofya Andreyevna's condition at that time really was such that she could have brought nothing to his death-bed but deception, vanity, material importunities, fuss and noise, that is well known by all who have had the opportunity of watching at close quarters her behaviour not only in all Leo Nikolaevitch's serious illnesses in later years and during the last months of his life at Yasnaya Polyana, but also during the first days after he had gone away, and during her stay in his neighbourhood at Astapovo, and by his bedside during the last unconscious moments, and during the first hours after his death. Anyone who saw Sofya Andreyevna under all these conditions cannot but acknowledge that Leo Nikolaevitch showed great foresight in so persistently avoiding interviews with her while she was in that condition. A personal interview between them at that time could not only add nothing to what he had told her in his last letters, which were permeated with forgiveness, pity and love, but, judging from the mental condition in which Sofya Andreyevna still was, it could only have evoked in her a renewal too painful for him of the same insincerity, hypocrisy and importunities which had provoked his departure.

64

CHAPTER X

THE SIGNIFICANCE OF TOLSTOY'S GOING AWAY AND OF THE WHOLE SPIRITUAL ACHIEVEMENT OF HIS LIFE

In an indirect way Leo Nikolaevitch's going away performed a great service in a social sense by manifesting clearly that his living beforehand for so long with his family was not due to the comforts of a rich man's life, nor to his weakness and lack of will where his wife was concerned. If circumstances had so fallen out that he had not left his family up to the day of his death, the value of the great example of his life would not, of course, have been one jot less in reality. But it would have been hard for many to believe that there was not a considerable share of egoism or weakness of character in his living with his wife in the surroundings in which his family lived. His departure from it revealed openly to contemporary and future generations that his life in Yasnaya Polyana really was surrounded by the most painful conditions. This event at once threw the true light on all that he must have suffered before that in his home surroundings, which many had been disposed to regard as peaceful and agreeable for him. Now it had become evident to all that Leo Nikolaevitch had remained with his family at Yasnaya Polyana for nearly thirty years after the whole manner of life had become distasteful and oppressive in the extreme for him,—and that he remained not at all because he wanted to enjoy the comfort of a wealthy landowner's life, nor because he was weak and wanting in will where his wife was concerned. Now it is easy to understand that during the whole of that time he was consciously sacrificing his preferences and inclinations for the sake of doing what he regarded as his duty to God and his family. And such an example of self-sacrifice and consistency on the part of such a man as Tolstoy doubtless has a conspicuous social value.

Many of the most various opinions have been expressed as to whether Tolstoy was right in leaving his family. To the friends of Leo Nikolaevitch who respected his soul and recognise the freedom of conscience and independence of human personality in all, the question in regard to Leo Nikolaevitch's going away is not whether he was right or wrong in taking that step. A man is really answerable not to the conscience of another, but only to his own. It is enough for us that it was not with a light heart that Leo Nikolaevitch came to his final decision to leave his wife. Once more I repeat that since he restrained himself for thirty years from going away, during the whole of that period patiently bearing the most poignant spiritual sufferings which often brought him to the verge of the grave,—and in the end he did die indeed from not having gone away sooner,—then surely we might do homage to the undoubted purity of his motives, and recognise that he had the right to decide the question in the end not in accordance with our views, but in accordance with his own judgment.

I at least for my part—carefully calling up before my imagination all that I heard with my own ears from Leo Nikolaevitch himself, and what I saw with my own eyes, amplifying this with what he wrote in his diary and said in various writings and intimate letters, and finally collating all this with contemporary communications, diaries and notes of most intimate friends who were, just as I was, witnesses of the great drama of the last months of his life—I do not see the possibility even from the most critical standpoint of seeing the slightest inconsistency in the fact that Leo Nikolaevitch remained so long with his wife and then thought it necessary to leave her. In this as in all else one can follow the inevitable, fully consistent and independent reaction of his inner life to external circumstances as they gradually opened out before him and suddenly took definite shape towards the end.

In all Leo Nikolaevitch's impulses and actions after the religious revolution which took place in him in the 'eighties, the same fundamental and guiding principle is all the time conspicuous; that is, the perpetual effort which persisted to the day of his death, to do not his own will nor the will of those surrounding him, but the will of God as he interpreted it according to his best understanding. What more can we expect of a man?

If some or other of Leo Nikolaevitch's actions during the last months of his life were not to the taste of some of his family, such, for instance, as his depriving them of the inheritance of his literary rights, his making a will without their knowledge and participation, his leaving his manuscripts and diaries to other people, and lastly his departing from amongst them; and if the material loss or their wounded vanity leads them mistakenly to ascribe all this to the supposed mental enfeeblement, the weakness of old age, and the fatal influence on him of the circle of his "followers," at least there is

67

no necessity for people who are in no way personally affected to follow the example of those of Leo Nikolaevitch's family who consider themselves injured and repeat their unfair charges, which come in reality to this, that Leo Nikolaevitch at the end of his life was in his dotage and did a whole series of bad and stupid things. Some of Leo Nikolaevitch's family wrongly imagined that since he had remained with his family so long he had lost all freedom of choice, and ought not to have moved from the spot until his death, like a thing laid on a shelf which cannot move of its own initiative. Leo Nikolaevitch was not only a living man, but a man of exceptionally strong and active inner life, which was continually growing and developing and spurring him on to new external manifestations which were often a surprise to those who watched him. On all the important occasions of his life he always acted without following any programme imposed on him from outside, or being affected by any personal influence; he was independently guided only by the prompting of his inner consciousness and entirely free from pose or any striving after effect. But at the same time he never drew back before the most extreme decisions when it was a question of obeying the dictates of his conscience. And so he had continually to do what was not foreseen or understood by others, and often not approved even by the majority of those about him.

At one time people were enthusiastic over Tolstoy's creative genius, and thought that he would do nothing all his life but write novels for them. He brooded over the meaning of life, devoted himself to the service of God, and began to point out to men how godlessly they lived. Then they, struck by his inspired indictment of social life, expected that he would abandon his family and go about the world preaching like a prophet. But, manifesting love first of all to

68

those nearest to him, and despising the censure of men, he remained almost thirty years with his wife and children under conditions most distressing for himself, hoping to be at least some little help in bringing them to a reasonable life. People became accustomed to the thought that old Tolstoy, physically weakened and professing the doctrine of non-resistance, would end his life at Yasnaya Polyana. But becoming convinced that being by his wife's side had in the end only become a stumbling-block to her and a restriction on his own spiritual life, to the surprise of all he left Yasnaya Polyana, at eighty-two, with shattered health, in order to live amidst poor surroundings, near to the working people so dear to his heart.

With Tolstoy everything was original and unexpected. The setting of his end was bound to be the same. Under the circumstances in which he was placed, and with the marvellously delicate sensitiveness and responsiveness to impressions which distinguished his exceptional nature, nothing else could or should have happened than just what did happen. There happened just what was in harmony with the external circumstances and the inner spiritual characteristics of Leo Nikolaevitch Tolstoy and no other. Any other solution of his domestic relations, any other surroundings of his death, even though in harmony with a certain traditional pattern, would have been false and artificial. Leo Nikolaevitch went away and died without affected sentimentality and emotional phrases, without loud words and eloquent gestures; he went away and died as he had lived, truthfully, sincerely and simply; and a better, truthful, more befitting end to his life could not be imagined, for just that end was the natural and inevitable one.

As time erases all the personal element which has hitherto played so great a part in the criticisms of Leo Nikolaevitch, all the purity of his impulses and deep wisdom of his decisions in the most complicated and difficult circumstances which could fall to the lot of man will stand out before the eyes of men in all their force. And then his life, especially its second period, from his spiritual awakening to his death, will serve as a bright and an increasing example of how we ought and can, guided by the voice of God in our souls, combine in our actions the greatest warmth of heart and gentleness toward those who injure us with an unalterable firmness where fidelity to that higher principle which one serves is concerned.

Telyatniki,
May 15th, 1913
Moscow, 1920

PART III

TOLSTOY'S ATTITUDE TO HIS SUFFERINGS

I think that to complete what has been said here about Tolstoy's "going away" it would be desirable to look rather more attentively at the growth of Leo Nikolaevitch's inner consciousness in the course of the last decades of his life, and at that side of the development of his spiritual life which is connected with his attitude to suffering, in particular to his own sufferings arising from the conditions of his family life which have been examined in the present book.

Let us listen first of all to Leo Nikolaevitch's own words in regard to the thoughts and feelings he had to pass through in this connection. For this purpose we make use of his diary and private letters. Much precious material on this subject is contained in his diary for 1884, which he personally handed to me to take care of immediately after it was finished, and from which I will make the following extracts. This diary was kept by Leo Nikolaevitch just at that time when the great drama of his family life, which in the end brought him to the tomb, was taking shape. I venture to give publicity to the lines quoted below, written by Leo Nikolaevitch in the most difficult moments of his life, solely for the sake of removing those misunderstandings and false deductions which, as I have indicated before, have accumulated in such numbers since his death around the question of his "going away." I hope that the reader will understand my motives and will approach these private notes of Leo Nikolaevitch with the same feeling of reverence with which I reproduce them here.

From the Diary of L. N. Tolstoy of 1884

April 16.—It is very painful at home, painful that I cannot sympathise with them. All their joys, examinations, successes in society, music, furniture, shopping, I look upon all of it as a misfortune and evil for them and cannot say that to them. I can and I do say it, but my words do not take hold of anyone. It seems as though they know not the meaning of my words, but that I have a bad habit of saying them. At weak moments—this is one now—I wonder at their heartlessness. How is it they do not see that, not to speak of suffering, I have had no life at all for these three years? I am given the part of a peevish old man and I cannot get out of it in their eyes. If I take part in their life I am false to the truth, and they will be the first to throw that in my face. If I look mournfully now upon their madness, I am a peevish old man like all old men.

April 23.—Shameful, disgusting. Terrible depression. I am all filled with weakness. I must as in a dream be on my guard so as not to spoil in the dream that which is needed for real life. I am drawn and drawn into the mire, and useless are my shudders. If only I am not drawn in without a protest! There has been no spite, little vanity, or none at all, but of weakness, mortal weakness, these days are full. Longing for real death. There is no despair. But I would like to live and not to be on guard on one's life.

April 24.—The same weakness and the same victorious mire sucking one in, drawing one down.

April 26.—Must be happy in an unhappy life, must ... make this the object of my life. And I can do it when I am strong in the spirit.

May 15.—I am miserable. I am an insignificant, useless creature, and am absorbed in myself besides. The one good thing is that I want to die.

May 16.—O Lord, save me from the hateful life which is crushing and destroying me. The one good thing is, I long to die. Better to die than live like this.

May 17.—I dreamed that my wife loved me. How light my heart was, everything grew bright. Nothing like it in reality. And that is destroying my life.... At home still the same general death. Only the little children are alive. A wearisome conversation at tea again. All one's life in terror.

May 26.—I am as in a dream ... when I know that a tiger is coming, and in a minute....

June 1.—Dullness, deadness of soul—that one could bear, but with it insolence, self-confidence ... one must know how to bear that too, if not with love, with pity. I am irritable, gloomy all day. I am bad.... How to live here, how to break through pouring sand. I will try.

June 2.—Conversation at tea with my wife. Angry again. Tried to write, it wouldn't go.... How be a shining light when I am still full of weakness which I have not the strength to overcome?

June 4.—Thought a great deal about my wife. I must love her and not be angry with her, must make her love me; so I will do.

June 6.—After dinner misery ... in the evening revived a little. Could not be loving as I would. I am very bad.

June 7.—I am trying to be bright and happy, but it is very, very hard. Everything I do is wrong, and I suffer horribly from this wrongness. It is as though I alone were not mad in the house of the mad managed by the mad.

June 9.—Agonising struggle, and I do not control myself. I look for the reasons—tobacco, incontinence, absence of imaginative work. It is all nonsense. The only cause is the absence of a loved and loving wife. It began from that time fourteen years ago when the cord snapped and I realised my loneliness.[26] All that is not a reason. I must find a wife in her. I ought, and I can and I will: Lord, help me.

June 10.—It is awful that the luxury, the corruption of life in which I live I have myself created, and I am myself corrupted and I cannot reform it. I can say that I shall reform myself, but so slowly. I cannot give up smoking, and I cannot find a way of treating my wife so as not to hurt her feelings and not to give in to her. I am seeking it, I am trying.

---

[26] To what precisely Leo Nikolaevitch ascribed his realisation that in 1870 the "cord had snapped" in the relations between him and his wife I am not in a position to state with certainty. I can only say for the information of the reader that I heard from Leo Nikolaevitch that their relations began to change for the worse from the time when Sofya Andreyevna, contrary to his principles and desire, refused to nurse her second daughter Marya Lvovna, born 1870, and engaged a wet nurse for her who was taken away from her own baby.

June 16.[27]—It was very painful, longed to go away at once. All that is weakness. Not for men's sake but for God's. Do as one knows best for oneself and not in order to prove something. But it is awfully painful. Of course I am to blame if it hurts me. I struggle, I put out the rising fire, but I feel that it has violently bent the scales. And indeed what use am I to them, what use are all my sufferings? And however hard (though they are easy) the conditions of a vagrant's life, there can be nothing in it like this heartache!

June 23.—I am calmer, stronger in spirit. In the evening a cruel conversation about the Samara revenues.[28] I am trying to act as though in the presence of God, and I cannot avoid anger. This must end.

July 6.—I was reading over the diary of those days when I was seeking the cause of temptation. All nonsense—it is the absence of hard physical labour.[29] I do not sufficiently prize the happiness of freedom from temptation after work. That happiness is cheaply bought at the price of fatigue and aching muscles.

July 5 (isn't it the 8th?).—My wife is very serene and contented and does not see the gulf between us. I try to do what I ought, but what I ought I do not know. I must do as I ought every minute, and everything will turn out as it should.

---

[27] It may interest the reader to know that on June 18 Sofya Andreyevna gave birth to her youngest daughter, Alexandra.—Translator's note.

[28] At that period Leo Nikolaevitch's attitude of disapproval of property was beginning to take definite shape. In consequence he did not wish to make use of the revenues from his estate in Samara, considering it unjust to make the peasants work for him and his family. Even the income which his family received from the Yasnaya Polyana estate and from the sale by Sofya Andreyevna of his works he considered as unjust, though he did not yet see clearly how he ought to act in the matter, considering his duties to his family.

[29] Compare entry for June 7.

July 19.—She came in to me and began a hysterical scene—the upshot of which is that nothing can be changed and she is unhappy and wants to run away somewhere. I was sorry for her, but at the same time I recognised that it was hopeless—to the day of my death she will be a millstone round my neck and my children's. I suppose it must be so. I must learn not to drown with a millstone round my neck. But the children? It seems it must be, and it only hurts me because I am short-sighted. I soothed her as though she were ill.

August 8.—I thought; we reproach God, we complain that we meet with obstacles in fulfilling the teaching of Christ. Well, but what if we were all free from families who disagree with us? We should come together and live happily and joyfully. But the others? The others would not know. We want to gather all the light together that it may burn better, but God has scattered the fire among the logs. They are being kindled while we fret that they are not burning.

August 12.—It is all right with my wife, but I am afraid and straining every nerve.

August 14.—Peace and friendliness with my wife, but I am afraid every minute.

August 20.—An outburst against me at dinner.... The sense of peace and welfare had got hold of the family. Every one depressed ... painful conversation in the house. Sonya, feeling that she was to blame tried to justify herself by anger. I was sorry for her.

August 21.—In the morning began a conversation, hotly too but well. I said what ought to be said.... I came home. Sonya was reconciled. How glad I was. Certainly if she would take to being good she would be very good.

September 3.—Something touches them somehow ... but I don't know how.

September 7.—Went looking for mushrooms ... my wife did not follow me but went off by herself not knowing where, only not after me—that is all our life.

September 9.—It is pleasant being with my wife. Told her unpleasant truths and she was not angry.

September 10.—Sonya tidied my room and then shouted disgustingly at Vlass. I am training myself to abstain from indignation and to see in it a moral bump which one must recognise as a fact and face its existence in one's action.

September 15.—Went to look for mushrooms. Miserable.

September 17.—Talk in the morning. And sudden fury. Then she came to me and nagged until I was beside myself. I said nothing and did nothing, but I was very unhappy. She ran away in hysterics, I ran after her, horribly worried.

After this diary of 1884 no diaries so far as I know were left by Leo Nikolaevitch for several years. Did he cease to keep his diary that he might not increase his spiritual sufferings by recording them on paper, preferring to continue his intense struggle with himself in complete solitude before no one but his God? Did he keep a diary and afterwards himself destroy it, not wishing to reveal to anyone the sufferings to which he was subjected? Were the missing diaries lost in some other way, if indeed they ever existed? To these questions there is no answer, and it is hardly likely there will be.

By Leo Nikolaevitch's notes in his later diaries kept from the year 1888, one thing is placed beyond doubt, that is, that his spiritual sufferings and inward struggles in connection with his family relations continued the whole of the rest of his life. And in this struggle his higher consciousness became brighter and brighter, his spiritual force grew and gained strength. As the years passed he gained an amazing mastery of his personal desires and weaknesses. At times, as indeed was inevitable, he recognised with peculiar pain his complete loneliness in the midst of the people surrounding him. To what degree he felt himself a stranger in his own family, how completely he was deprived of that warm, genuine sympathy on the part of his wife which is the most precious thing in married life, can to some extent be judged by the notes in which, with irrepressible grief, he recalls his mother.

His attitude to her memory, as is well known, was always the most reverent. In his Recollections of Childhood he writes of her: "It was necessary for her to love not herself, and one love followed another. Such is the spiritual figure of my mother in my imagination; she stood before me as such a lofty, pure, spiritual being that often in the middle period of my life, when I was struggling with temptations which almost overwhelmed me, I prayed to her soul, entreating her to help me, and this prayer was always a help to me."

Leo Nikolaevitch sometimes invoked the holy image of his mother in his most difficult moments, even in his old age. In the beginning of 1900 he wrote on a scrap of paper, "Dull, miserable state the whole day. Towards evening this mood passed into tenderness—a desire for fondness, for love, longed as children do to press up to a loving, pitying creature and to weep with emotion and to be comforted. But what creature is there to whom I could come close like that? I go over all the people I have loved; not one is suitable to whom I can come close. If I could be little and snuggle up to my mother as I imagine her to myself! Yes, yes, mother whom I called to when I could not speak, yes, she, my highest imagination of pure love,—not cold, divine love, but earthly, warm, motherly. It is to that that my battered, weary soul is drawn. You, mother, you caress me. All this is senseless, but it is all true."

On apparently the next day, calmly analysing the attack of misery he had passed through the day before, he wrote in his diary: "Yesterday particularly oppressed condition. Everything unpleasant felt with peculiar vividness. So I say to myself, but in reality I seek what is unpleasant; I am receptive, absorbent to what is unpleasant. I could not get rid of this feeling anyhow. I have tried everything—prayer and the sense of my own badness—and nothing succeeds. Prayer, that is, vividly picturing my position does not reach to the depths of my consciousness; the recognition of my worthlessness, paltriness does not help. It is not that one wants something, but is miserably dissatisfied one does not know with what. It seems it is with life, one longs to die. Towards evening this condition passed into a feeling of forlornness and an overwhelming desire of fondling, of love; I, an old man, longed to be a baby, to snuggle up to a loving creature, to be petted, to complain and to be fondled and comforted. But who is the being to whom I could snuggle up and on whose arms I could weep and complain? There is no one living. Then what is this? Still the same devil of egoism which in such a new, cunning form is trying to deceive and overpower me. This last feeling has explained to me the state of misery which preceded it. It is only the weakening, the temporary disappearance of spiritual life and the assertion of the claims of egoism which on awakening finds no food for itself and is miserable. The only means to use against it is to serve someone in the simplest way that comes first, to work for someone."—(Diary, March 11, 1906.)

The complete absence in Leo Nikolaevitch of the slightest sentimentality in regard to the spiritual sufferings which he had to endure was apparently connected with his lofty conception of Christ and the deep reverence he felt for his heroic life. In 1885 Leo Nikolaevitch wrote: "Christ conquered the world and saved it not by suffering for us, but by suffering with love and joy, i.e. by conquering suffering, and he taught us thereby."

And indeed to the very last days and hours of his life Leo Nikolaevitch persistently and with striking success strove to train himself to "conquer suffering." In confirmation of my words I quote a series of further extracts from his diaries and letters.

June 15, 1889 (from a diary).—"I am burdened by life, I forget that if one has vital forces they can be used for the service of God, and that there is no getting away, there is no emptiness, everywhere there is contact, and in contact there is life."

July 18, 1889 (from the letters).—"What do I want? To live with God, according to His will, with Him. What is wanted for that? One thing only is wanted: to preserve the talent given to me, my soul, given to me not only to preserve but to make it grow. How make it grow? I know for myself what is needed; to keep what is animal in me in purity, what is human in humility, and what is divine in love. What is wanted for preserving purity? Privations, privations of every sort. Humility? humiliation. Love? the hostility of men. Where and how am I to keep my purity without privations, my humility without humiliation, and my love without hostility? 'And if you love those that love you, that is not love, but love ye your enemies, love ye those that hate you.' One sorrow approaches humiliation and hostility, and these thoughts have revived me. Another sorrow is privation, suffering—the very thing that is needed for the growth of the soul. That is how one must look at it."

July 18, 1889 (from the letters).—All our sorrows have one root, and, strange as it sounds, they all not only can, but ought, to be a blessing.... God grant that we may believe in the possibility of it— that is one thing; and the other is that we may not return in thought to our sorrow, in our imagination changing the conditions in which our sorrow has occurred and correcting our actions. "If we had done this or that this would not have happened." God preserve us from this mistake, with its painful consequences. What has been is, and what is was bound to have been, and all our vital force ought to be directed to the present, to bearing our cross in the best way possible.

December, 1889 (from the letters).—The cross is given according to the strength.... I believe that, and cannot but believe it, because I know by experience that the harder my sufferings have been, if only I have succeeded in taking them in a Christian spirit ... the fuller, more vivid, more joyful and full of meaning life has become. It is so often insincerely repeated that sufferings are good for us and are sent by God, that we have ceased to believe it, and yet it is the simplest, clearest and most indubitable truth. Suffering—what is called suffering—is the condition of spiritual growth. Without suffering growth is impossible, the widening of life is impossible. For this reason sufferings also always accompany death. If a man had no suffering he would be in a bad way; that is why they say among the people that those whom God loves He visits by misfortunes. I understand that a man may be sad and apprehensive when misfortunes have not visited him for a long time. There is no movement, no growth of life. Suffering is only suffering for the heathen, for the man who has not the light of the truth, and for us in the measure in which we have not the light; but sufferings cease to be such for the Christian—they become birth-pangs, even as Christ promised to deliver us from evil. And all this is not rhetoric,

81

but is for me as undoubtedly in accordance with reason and experience as that it is now winter.

1892-3 (from the letters).—Nothing, I imagine, sets a man free from dependence on others and brings him near, or rather may bring him near, to God so much as your position. One only leans upon Him when men compel one to. God help you to bear your cross patiently, submissively, so as to get from it all the good which external suffering gives and can give. Or it will be mortifying that there has been suffering, but struggling with it, indignant and despairing, you did not get from it all that it is capable of giving.

May 17, 1893 (from the letters).—I am forced to live without personal, legitimate joys such as you have: labour, associations with animals, nature; without association (not poisoned by their corruption) with children; without the encouragement of public opinion. What has happened to me is not exactly that the praise of men has destroyed for me the attractiveness of their praise, but their praise has been tainted, has become poisoned. I cannot now desire the praise of men, fame among the crowd, because I have it and know how double-faced it is; if there are some who praise, there are others who revile; that praise of men which you have, the good opinion of estimable men for a good life, at least consistent with your convictions I cannot have. And on the top of all that this praise of men—the way they write abroad and the opinion is current, that I lead a modest, laborious life in poverty—that praise arraigns me every second as a liar, a scoundrel living in luxury, making money out of the sale of his books. If I think of the praise of men it is like a thief who is every minute afraid that he will be caught, so that I have not only to live without the stimulus of lawful joys, and not only without the praise of men, but even with the perpetual consciousness of the shamefulness of life; I have to live by

82

that which I consider men can and ought to live by; that is, by the consciousness of fulfilling the will of Him who sent us. And I see that I am still far from being ready for that, and am still only learning, and life is teaching me. And I ought to rejoice, and I do rejoice.

February 28, 1894 (from the letters).—The longer I live and the nearer I am to death, the more certain to me is the injustice of our wealthy mode of life, and I cannot help suffering by it.

March 27, 1895 (from a diary).—If there is suffering there has been and is egoism. Love does not know suffering, because the loving life is the divine life which can do all. Egoism is the limitation of personality.

December 20, 1896 (from a diary).—Everything just as painful. Help me, O Father. Comfort me. Be strong in me, subdue me, drive out and destroy the unclean flesh and all that I feel through it. It is better now though. Particularly soothing is the problem—the trial of meekness, of humiliation, of quite unexpected humiliation. In fetters, in prison one may be proud of humiliation, but in this case it is merely painful, unless one takes it as a trial sent from God. Yes, I will learn to bear it calmly, joyfully and to love.

January 18, 1897 (from a diary).—Depressing, disgusting. Everything repels me in the life they are living around me. Alternately I get free from misery and suffering and fall into it again. Nothing shows so clearly how far I am from what I want to be. If my life really were spent wholly in the service of God nothing could trouble it.

April 4, 1907 (from a diary).—I have not lost my calm though my soul is agitated, but I am mastering it. O God! if one could but remember that one is His messenger, that the divinity ought to shine through one! But what is hard is that if one only remembers this, one will not live, and yet one must live, live energetically and remember. Help me O Father. I have prayed a great deal of late that life might be better, for I am ashamed and cast down by the consciousness of the unrighteousness of my life.

July 12, 1897 (from the letters).—I understand your trouble and sympathise with all my heart. It is your examination, try not to fail in it. Remember that it is the one chance of applying your faith to life. I always strengthen myself with that in difficult moments, and sometimes with success.

1897 (from the letters).—The doubts as to whether one makes concessions for the sake of not destroying love or for the sake of indulging in one's own weaknesses persist as ever, and the older I get, the more strongly I feel this sin, and I humble myself, but I do not submit, and I hope to rise up again.

March 10, 1899 (from the letters).—It is very difficult and dreary and lonely for me and I am afraid of unpleasantness—of people being angry with me, and people are angry with me.

November 29, 1901 (from a diary).—If you are suffering it is only from your not seeing everything (the time has not yet come). What is accomplished by those sufferings has not been revealed.

January 31, 1903 (from the letters).—Sufferings are profitable just because a man in ordinary worldly life forgets the unbreakable bond which exists between all living creatures; the sufferings which he endures and of which he has been the cause to other people remind him of that bond. This bond is spiritual, seeing that the Son of God is one in all men; physical sufferings drive a man

84

involuntarily into the spiritual sphere in which he feels in union with God and with the world, and in which he ... bears the sufferings caused by others as though caused by himself, and even joyfully takes upon himself the burden of suffering, taking it from others. In that is the profit and fruitfulness of suffering.

June 12, 1905 (from a diary).—More and more I am pained by my abundance and the want surrounding me.

May 29, 1906 (from a diary).—I am very heavy-hearted with shame at my life, and what to do I don't know: Lord, help me.

November 23, 1906 (from a diary).—In a very good spiritual state of love for all. Read the Epistle of St. John. Marvellous, only now I understand it fully. To-day there was a great temptation which I did not fully conquer. Abakumov overtook me with a petition and a complaint at having been sentenced to prison on account of the oak trees. It was very painful. He cannot understand that I, the husband, cannot do as I like, and looks on me as an evil-doer and a Pharisee hiding behind my wife. I had not the strength to bear it lovingly, said that I could not go on living here. And that was wrong. Altogether I am more and more abused on all hands; that's a good thing, it drives me to God—if I could only remain there. Altogether I am conscious of one of the greatest changes which has taken place in me just now. I feel this from my serenity and joyfulness and the good feeling (I dare not say love) for people.

June 7, 1907 (from a diary).—My former ailment has passed, but a new one seems to be beginning. To-day I was very, very sad. I am ashamed to confess it, but I cannot call up joy. My soul is calm and grave, but not joyful. My sadness is chiefly due to the darkness in which people live so persistently. The exasperation of the peasants, our senseless luxury. Experienced the joy of being alone with God

... sorrowful, sorrowful. Lord, help me, burn up the old fleshly man in me. Yes, the one consolation, the one salvation is to live in eternity and not in time.

April 7, 1908 (from the letters).—One thing I can say, that the reasons which restrain me from changing my manner of life as you advise me,—though not changing it, is a source of misery to me— the reasons that hinder me have their origin in the same principles of love, in the name of which the change is desirable both for you and me. It is very probable that I do not know and am not capable, or simply there are bad qualities in me which prevent me from doing what you advise me. But what is to be done? With the utmost effort of my mind and heart I cannot find the means, and I should only be thankful to anyone who will point it out to me. I say this quite sincerely, without any irony.

May 20, 1908 (from a diary).—My life is good in that I bear all the burden of a wealthy life which I detest—the sight of others labouring for me, the begging for help, the censure, the envy, the hatred,—and I do not enjoy its advantages, even that of loving what is done for me and helping those who ask.

July 3, 1908 (from a diary).—The day before yesterday I received a letter full of upbraidings for my wealth and hypocrisy and persecution of the peasants, and, to my shame, it hurt me. To-day I have been sad and ashamed all day. Just now I went for a ride, and it seemed so desirable, so joyful to go away like a beggar, thanking and loving everyone. Yes, I am weak, I cannot perpetually live in my spiritual self, and as soon as one does not live in it, everything vexes one. One thing is good, that I am dissatisfied with myself and ashamed, but I must not be proud of it.

July 9, 1908 (from a diary).—I have passed through very painful feelings; thank God that I have passed through them. An innumerable multitude of people, and all this would be joyful if it were not all poisoned by the consciousness of the senselessness, sinfulness, nastiness, luxury, servants, and poverty and overstrained intensity of labour around. Without ceasing I suffer misery from it, and I alone. I cannot help wishing for death, though I hope as far as I can to make use of what is left.

January 12, 1909 (from a diary).—It grows more and more difficult. I do not know how to thank God that, together with the growing difficulty, the strength to endure it grows also. Together with the burden there is also the strength, and there is incomparably more joy from the consciousness of strength than pain from the burden. Yes, for His yoke is easy and His burden is light.

May 6, 1907 (from the letters).—It is hard for you. God help you to bear your trial without reproaches to others and without infringement of love for them. It is always a great help to me, when anything is difficult, to think and to remember that it is the material—and necessary, good material—upon which I am called to work, and not before men but before God.

July 21, 1909 (from a diary).—Last night Sonya has been weak and irritable. I could not go to sleep till after two o'clock. I woke up feeling weak, I was awakened. Sonya did not sleep all night. I went to her. It was something insane. "Dushan poisoned her," etc. I am tired and cannot stand it any more and feel quite ill. I feel I cannot be loving and reasonable, absolutely cannot. At present I want only to keep away and to take no part. There is nothing else I can do, or else I have seriously thought of escaping. Now then, show your Christianity. C'est le moment ou jamais. But I awfully want to go away. I doubt if my presence here is of any use to anyone. Help me, my God, teach me. There is only one thing I want—to do not my

87

will, but Thine. I write and ask myself: Is it true? Am I posing to myself? Help me, help me, help me!

July 22, 1909 (from a diary).—Yesterday I did not eat anything and did not sleep. As usual I felt very wretched. I am wretched now, but my heart is melted. Yes—to love those that do us evil, you say; will try it. I try, but badly. I think more and more of going away and making a settlement about property.... I don't know what I shall do. Help, help, help! This "help" means that I am weak, bad. It is a good thing that I am at any rate conscious of this....

July 26, 1909 (from a diary).—After dinner I spoke of Sweden; she became terribly, hysterically irritated. She wanted to poison herself with morphia. I tore it out of her hands and threw it under the stairs. I struggled. But when I went to bed and thought it over calmly I decided not to go. I went and told her. She is pitiful; I am truly sorry for her. But how instructive it is! I did nothing except inwardly work at myself. And as soon as I started on my own self, everything was solved. I have been ill all day....

August 28, 1909 (from a diary).—Dreadfully, dreadfully miserable and oppressed; depression partly produced by letter from Berlin, in reference to Sofya Andreyevna's letter and the article in the Petersburg News, saying that Tolstoy is a deceiver and a hypocrite. To my shame I did not rejoice at being reviled, but was hurt, and the whole evening was agonisingly depressed. Go away? More and more often the question presents itself.

August 29, 1909 (from a diary).—Painful feeling and desire (a bad one?) to run away, and uncertainty what is my duty to God. In calm moments, as now, I know that what is necessary above all is to do nothing, to bear all, to remain in love.

September 4, 1909 (from a diary).—The false judgment of men about me, the necessity for remaining in this position—however hard it all is, I begin at times to understand its beneficial effect on my soul.

November 15, 1909 (from a diary).—The misery, almost despair, at my idle life in senseless luxury, in the midst of men who are overworked and deprived of the essentials, of the possibility of satisfying their first needs, keeps growing more intense. It is agonising to live like this, and I do not know how to help myself and them. In weak moments I long to die. Help me, O Father, to do Thy will up to the last minute. Meditation about myself which I am learning, and to which I am giving myself up more and more of late, has advanced me much, very much; but, as always, true progress in goodness ... only reveals one's imperfection more and more.

January 8, 1910 (from the letters).—I live wrongly in wealth, though myself I have nothing, but with those who live in wealth.

January 8, 1910 (from the letters).—If man grows weak he is weaker than water. If he grows strong he is stronger than rock. What strengthens me most in difficult moments is the sense that the very thing that is worrying one is the material on which we are called to work, and the material is the more precious the more difficult the moments.

March 19, 1910 (from the letters).—In bad moments think that what is happening to you is the material on which you are called to work. To me at any rate this thought and the feeling evoked by it is a great help.

April 13, 1910 (from a diary).—I woke at five and kept thinking how to get out, what to do, and I don't know. I thought of writing—and writing is loathsome while I remain in this life. Speak to her? Go away? Change? By degrees ... it seems as though the last is the only thing I shall and can do, and yet it is painful. Perhaps, certainly, indeed that is good. Help me, Thou Who art in me, in everything, and Who exists and Whom I implore and love. I am weeping now as I love.

April 14, 1910 (from the letters).—You ask whether I like the life in which I find myself. No, I don't like it. I don't like it because I am living with my own people in luxury while there are poverty and want around me, and I cannot get away from the luxury, and I cannot help the poverty and want. For this I do not like my life. I like it in that it is in my power to act, and that I can act, and that I do act in the measure of my strength in accordance with the teaching of Christ, to love God and my neighbour. To love God means to love the perfection of goodness and to approach it as far as one can. To love one's neighbour is to love all people alike as one's brothers and sisters. It is this, and this alone, that I am striving for, and since, little by little, however poorly, I am approaching it I do not grieve, but only rejoice. You ask me too, if I rejoice, at what do I rejoice, and what joy do I expect? I rejoice that I can carry out to the measure of my strength the task set me by my Master; to work for the setting up of that Kingdom of God to which we are all striving.

June 4, 1910 (from a diary).—I had a good ride; I came back and found the Circassian who was taking Prokofy. I was horribly distressed and thought of going away, and now at five in the morning I don't look on that as impossible.

July 2, 1910 (from the letters).—All will be well if we do not grow weak.... Very painful, but the better for that.

July 16, 1910 (from the letters).—I feel well ... a little weaker than usual, but still well.... Why, really when I am calm I actually feel that in all this there is more of good than bad, incomparably more. It is absurd even to compare the little unpleasantnesses, agitations, privations, and the sense of growing nearer to God.

July 20, 1910 (from the letters).—I am grateful to you for having helped and helping me to bear the trial that I have deserved and that is needful for my soul.... And please do help us both not to grow weak and not to do anything of which we shall repent.

July 29, 1910 (from the letters).—We will each of us try to act as we ought, and it will be all right. I am trying with all my might, and I feel that that is the only thing that matters.

July 31, 1910 (from the letters).—If only we do not ourselves spoil things all will be as it ought to be—that is, well.

August 7, 1910 (from the letters).—I am sorry for her, and she is undoubtedly more to be pitied than I, so that it would be wrong of me to increase her sufferings out of pity for myself. Though I am tired I am really all right. Ever nearer and nearer comes the revelation of the certainly blessed, fore-divined mystery, and getting near it cannot but rejoice me.

August 9, 1910 (from the letters).—The nearer one is to death, or anyway the more vividly one thinks of it (and thinking of it is thinking of one's own true life which is independent of death), the more important the one needful work of life becomes, and the clearer it is that for the securing of that non-infringement of love with anyone, I must not undertake anything, but only do nothing.

August 14, 1910, morning (from the letters).—I know that all this present particularly morbid state may seem affected, intentionally worked up (to some extent that is so), but the chief point is that it is anyway illness, perfectly obvious illness, that deprives her of will and self-control. If it is said that she is herself to blame for this relaxation of her will, for giving in to her egoism, which began long ago, the fault is of the past, of long ago. Now she is quite irresponsible and one can feel for her nothing but pity, and it is impossible, for me at any rate, utterly impossible, contrecourir (to run counter to) her, and so unmistakably increase her sufferings. I do not believe that the complete vindication of my decision opposed to her wishes would be good for her, and if I did believe it I still could not do that. Apart from the fact that I think that I ought to act in this way, the point is that I know from experience that when I insist, I am miserable, and when I give way I am not only light-hearted, I am even joyful.... I have been ill for the last few days, but to-day I am much better. And I am particularly glad of it to-day, because there is anyway fewer chances of one's saying or doing wrong when one is physically well.

August 14, 1910, evening (from the letters).—I agree that one ought not to make promises to anyone, and especially to a person in the state in which she is now, but I am bound now not by any promise, but simply by pity, by compassion, which I have been feeling particularly strongly to-day as I wrote to you. Her position is very painful, no one can see it and not sympathise with it.

August 20, 1910; Kotchety. (From the letters.)—Without exaggeration I can say that I recognise that what has happened was inevitable, and therefore profitable for my soul. I think so at any rate in my better moments.

August 25, 1910; Kotchety. (From the letters.)—Of myself I may say that I am very well here, even my health, which was affected too by agitation, is far better. I am trying to behave as justly and firmly as possible in regard to Sofya Andreyevna, and it seems as though I am more or less successful in my object of calming her.... I am often terribly sorry for her. When one thinks what it must be for her lying awake alone at nights, for she gets no sleep for the greater part of the night, with a confused but painful consciousness that she is not loved, but is burdensome to everyone except the children, one cannot but pity her.

August 28, 1910; Kotchety. (From the letters.)—Do not think that it is easy for me to advise the manly, serene and even joyful endurance of suffering because I do not myself experience it. Do not think that, because all men are liable to sufferings which may be regarded as objectless torments, or as trials, the mild and religious endurance of which may, strange as it sounds, be transmuted to a greater spiritual blessing. We are all liable to these trials, and often to much harder ones than those which you are enduring. May God who lives in you help you to be conscious of yourself. And when there is that consciousness there is no suffering and there is no death.

August 30, 1910; Kotchety. (From the letters.)—Sofya Andreyevna went away from here yesterday, and took a very touching farewell of me and Tanya and her husband, with evident sincerity begging forgiveness of all with tears in her eyes. She is inexpressibly pathetic. What will happen later I cannot imagine. "Do what you ought before your conscience and God, and what will be will be," I say to myself and try to act on it.

September 9, 1910; Kotchety. (From the letters.)—She was very much irritated, not irritated (ce n'est pas le mot, that is not the right word), but morbidly agitated. I underline that word. She is unhappy and cannot control herself. I have only just been talking to her. She came thinking I should go away with her, but I have

93

refused without fixing the date of my going away, and that greatly distressed her. What I shall do later I don't know. I shall try to bear my cross day by day.

September 16, 1910 (from the letters).—I am still as before in a middling condition physically, and spiritually I try to look upon my painful or rather difficult relations with Sofya Andreyevna as a trial which is good for me, and which it depends upon myself to turn into a blessing, but I rarely succeed in this. One thing I can say: not in my brain but with my sides, as the peasants say, I have come to a clear understanding of the difference between resistance which is returning evil for evil, and the resistance of not giving way in those of one's actions which one recognises as one's duty to one's conscience and to God. I will try.

September 18, 1910 (from the letters).—I understand now from experience that all that we call suffering is for our good.

October 6, 1910 (from the letters).—She is ill and all the rest of it, but it is impossible not to pity her and not to be indulgent to her.

October 17, 1910 (from the letters).—Yesterday was a very serious day. Others will describe the physical details to you, but I want to give you my own account from the inside. I pity and pity her, and rejoice that at times I love her without effort. It was so last night when she came in penitent and began seeing about warming my room, and in spite of her exhaustion and weakness pushed the shutters and screened the windows, taking pains and trouble about my ... bodily comfort. What's to be done if there are people for whom, and I believe only for a time, the reality of spiritual life is unattainable. Yesterday evening I was almost on the point of going away to Kotchety, but now I am glad I did not go. To-day I feel physically weak, but serene in spirit.

94

October 26, 1910 (from a diary).—It is very oppressive for me in this house of lunatics.

October 26, 1910 (from the letters).—The third thing is not so much a thought as a feeling, and a bad feeling—the desire to change my position. I feel something unbefitting, rather shameful, in my position. Sometimes I look upon it as I ought, as a blessing but sometimes I struggle against it and am revolted....

October 27, 1910 (from a diary).—It seems bad but is really good; the oppressiveness of our relations keeps increasing.

October 29, 1910 (from the letters).—I am waiting to see what will come of the family deliberation—I think, good. In any case, however, my return to my former life has become still more difficult—almost impossible, owing to the reproaches which will now be showered upon me, and the still smaller share of kindness which will be shown me. I cannot and will not enter into any sort of negotiations—what will be will be—only to sin as little as possible.... I cannot boast of my physical and spiritual condition, they are both weak and shattered. I feel most of all sorry for her. If only that pity were quite free from an admixture of rancune (resentment), and that I cannot boast of.

October 29, 1910; Optin Monastery. (From a diary.)—I have been much depressed all day and physically weak.... As I came here I was thinking all the time on the road, of the way out of my and her position, and could not think of any way out of it, but yet there will be one whether one likes it or not; it will come, and not be what one foresees. Yes, think only of how to avoid sin, and let come what will come. That is not my affair. I have taken up ... the Circle of Reading, and, just now, reading Number Twenty-eight was struck by the direct answer to my position: trial is what I need, it is beneficial for me. I am going to bed at once. Help me, O Lord.

November 3, 1910; Station Astapovo. (From a diary; the last words written by Leo Nikolaevitch in his diary.)—Fais ce que doit adv....[30] And it is all for the best both for others and for me.

The extracts from the diary and letters of Tolstoy that have been quoted, though far from exhausting all the material, show sufficiently clearly what Leo Nikolaevitch had to endure in connection with his family and domestic conditions in the course of the last thirty years of his life. In it of course all aspects of his spiritual growth are not touched upon, the whole course of his inner development during that period is not explained. But what is revealed to us in these extracts is sufficient to excite the warmest sympathy for Leo Nikolaevitch in his great and prolonged ordeal, and to inspire the deepest respect for his touching ability to blame himself for everything, and always to strive not towards what he desired but towards his duty. At the same time there is here revealed to us in its general features the path by which he came to the conviction that if we suffer spiritually we are ourselves to blame.

As is the case with everyone for whom the true meaning of life is revealed, after Leo Nikolaevitch's inner awakening at the beginning of the 'eighties, his spiritual consciousness could not, of course, remain at the same point. And indeed from the fragments we have quoted we see that up to the very last days of his life it was growing and becoming more perfect, as he became more and more penetrated with purity and strength.

Becoming convinced that in spite of all his sufferings he could not draw his wife to take part in his efforts, Leo Nikolaevitch began to

[30] An unfinished French proverb; translated in full it means, "Do what you ought and let come what may."

96

experience the most agonising distress, which, as we see from his diary of 1884, sometimes became so acute that he hardly had the strength to endure it. He even had moments almost of despair and as it were revolt against his fate, especially when he learned from experience that his wife was too far away from him spiritually to be his companion in the reorganisation of their lives. It was at such a moment that there broke from him that agonising cry of a tortured heart, that she would for ever remain a millstone round his neck and his children's. But at the same time he tried to accept these sufferings with meekness and submission as a trial laid upon him, and to behave with love and patience to her who evoked them. So about the same time, on one of those exceptionally rare occasions when in conversation with me he permitted himself to touch on his relations with his wife, he spoke approximately as follows:

"It is impossible to blame Sofya Andreyevna. It is not her fault that she does not follow me. Why, what she clings to so obstinately now is the very thing in which I trained her for many years. Apart from that, in the early days of my awakening I was too irritable and insisted on trying to convince her that I was right. In those days I put my new conception of life before her in a form so repellent and unacceptable to her that I quite put her off. And now I feel that through my own fault she can never come to the truth by my way. That door is closed for her. But, on the other hand, I notice with joy that by ways peculiar to her alone, and quite incomprehensible to me, she seems at times to be gradually moving in the same direction."

About the same time Leo Nikolaevitch wrote to me:

"'He who loves not his brother, he dwelleth in death.' I have learned, but to my cost. I did not love, I had malice against my

97

neighbours, and I was dying and dead. I began to be afraid of death; not afraid exactly, but bewildered before it. But love had but to rise up and I rose up again. I had forgotten Christ's first precept, 'Be not wrathful.' So simple, so small and so immense! If there is one man whom one does not love one is lost, one is dead. I have learned that by experience."—(Letter, December 28, 1885.)

At that period of his life Leo Nikolaevitch wrote in his diary the reflection which has already appeared in print concerning the chloroform of love, which expresses with remarkable vividness his recognition of the way we ought to help men who have gone astray: "At first I thought, Can one point out to people their mistakes, their sins, their faults, without hurting them? We have chloroform and cocaine for physical pain, but not for the soul. I thought this, and at once it came into my head, it is untrue—there is such a spiritual chloroform. They perform the operation of amputating a leg or an arm with chloroform, but they perform the operation of reforming a man painfully, stifling the reform with pain, exciting the worse disease—vindictiveness. But there is a spiritual chloroform, and it has long been known,—always the same—love. And that is not all: in physical disease one may do good by an operation without chloroform, but the soul is such a sensitive creature that an operation performed upon it without the chloroform of love is never anything but injurious. Patients always know it and ask for chloroform, and know that it ought to be used.... The sick man is in pain and he screams, hides the sore spot and says, 'You won't heal me, you won't heal me, and I don't want to be healed, I would rather get worse if you cannot heal me without pain....' And he is right ... you cannot drag a man straight out when he is tangled in a net—you will hurt him. You must disentangle the netting gently and firmly first. This delay, this disentangling, is the chloroform of love.... This I almost understood before, now I quite understand and begin to feel it...."

(Tolstoy's diary, January 25, 1889. Cf. Biography of L. N. Tolstoy by P. I. Biryukov, Vol. III. chap. iii.)

Striving to work out in himself a patient and loving attitude to the erring, beginning with those who were nearest to him, Leo Nikolaevitch from the earliest days of his domestic ordeal applied all his spiritual forces to avoiding giving way to his spiritual sufferings and throwing the blame for them either on people or on external circumstances. And this consciousness was continually strengthened and confirmed in him, helping him to bestow less and less pity on himself and more and more pity on those at whose hands he suffered. At first, as we have seen, such resignation to destiny was attained only with the greatest spiritual effort; but gradually he succeeded in conquering himself more and more by means of this incessant struggle carried on for many years. Such, anyway, is, it seems to me, the general deduction which may be drawn from his diary and letters. This deduction is confirmed too by the immediate impression which many of those to whose lot it fell to be in close relations with Leo Nikolaevitch in his later years carried away from personal intercourse with him. Even the expression of his face during this last period often seemed lighted up with a peculiar spiritual radiance. Such in its most general features is my conception of the consistent growth of Leo Nikolaevitch's inner consciousness after his spiritual awakening in so far as that growth is connected with his domestic sufferings and going away from home. This conception has been formed, on the one hand, on the basis of my personal intimacy and my spiritual unity with Leo Nikolaevitch as well as my long, intimate acquaintance with his family; and, on the other hand, on an attentive study of all that Leo Nikolaevitch has at various times expressed in his letters.

But the secret of another man's soul is too great and too intricate for anyone to be able to assert with confidence that he has fully grasped it even on any one side. And therefore while expressing here my personal opinion so far as it can have significance for anyone, I feel great satisfaction in the fact that I have been able to a considerable extent to incorporate Leo Nikolaevitch's own words in this book. And thus it will be possible for the reader to draw his own conclusions; at least from those notes of Leo Nikolaevitch's which I have here brought into connection with my argument, and to correct for himself anything in which it may seem to him that I am mistaken. I should like to conclude with two more thoughts of Leo Nikolaevitch's which show his comprehension of the spiritual significance of suffering.

"For a man living a spiritual life suffering is always an encouragement to becoming more perfect and more enlightened, and getting nearer to God. For such people suffering can always be transformed into the business of life."—(Circle of Reading.)

"The cross that is laid upon us is that at which we ought to work. Our whole life is this work. If the cross is illness, then bear it well, with submission; if it is injury at the hands of men, know how to return good for evil; if it is humiliation, be meek; if it is death, accept it with gratitude."—(The Way of Life.)

APPENDIX I

In view of the fact that Leo Nikolaevitch's diaries and letters have not yet been published in their entirety, I think it essential to make a note in connection with the character of the extracts which I have made from them in this book. These passages have been selected with the special object of illustrating Leo Nikolaevitch's attitude to suffering in general and to his own sufferings in particular. Owing to this, their context is inevitably one-sided and cannot give a general idea of his prevailing spiritual mood during the last thirty years of his life. That general mood, in spite of the conditions which oppressed Leo Nikolaevitch externally, was doubtless one of joy in life, in accordance with the characteristics of his nature, and filled with inner satisfaction, as all those who were in close communication with him for any length of time during that period can testify. And in this fact, i.e. in his preserving those characteristics in spite of all the trials to which he was subjected throughout that whole period, I see one of the most remarkable aspects of his heroic endurance.

Indeed one has but for one moment to enter in spirit into his position at that time to be truly amazed at what he succeeded in attaining in his inner life. Love for freedom in general and for personal independence was to an exceptional degree characteristic of his powerful personality. The demands of creative work attracted him to prolonged absences far from home in the midst of the most varied natural scenery, and the most different strata of humanity. The working of his mind after his spiritual awakening required the closest association with working people. For the satisfaction of his spiritual needs he required the possibility of receiving unhindered in his house all and each of those with whom he would have liked to hold intercourse, without any limitation or restriction, and consequently to show hospitality, to seat at his table on occasions, to put up for the night both the peasant of the district who had come to pay him a visit, and the passing pilgrim weary from the road, and the visitor who had come from afar seeking spiritual intercourse and help.... And of all this so needful to Tolstoy as artist and thinker, and above all as a man leading a spiritual life,—of all this he was deprived, thanks to the egoism of his family and the class prejudices ruling in his house, in which a woman's self-will was paramount. Being completely indifferent to his spiritual needs and callous to his sufferings, Sofya Andreyevna expected him in his old age, as in the first period of their life, to be continually at her side in spite of the spiritual change that had taken place in her husband, and only rarely agreed to his being absent for short intervals, and then with the greatest difficulty. Leo Nikolaevitch could not refuse these demands of hers without destroying the very small share of domestic peace without which his life in the home would have lost any sort of meaning. And in spite of all the oppressiveness of these domestic conditions, which defy description in words and, lasting as they did over thirty years, for us ordinary people would have been truly shattering, Leo Nikolaevitch, far from giving way to despair, did not even complain of his fate. On the contrary, he blamed himself for his sufferings, ascribing them to his own imperfection, and making the utmost effort to perform his family duties as irreproachably as possible. "I am all right, quite all right," he often said and wrote to his friends. At times he even displayed a childlike gaiety, and sometimes jested at the very circumstances which caused him the most suffering.

This remarkable circumstance I explain solely by the fact that Leo Nikolaevitch firmly made it his aim to do nothing but the will of God. This, and only this, he set before him as his fundamental task, and for the sake of carrying it out he consciously denied himself the satisfaction of his personal needs and any self-gratification during the whole of that second long period of his married life. And denying himself all the so-called joys of life, he incidentally attained true spiritual joy and peace, true blessedness.

The subject of Leo Nikolaevitch's inner life is, however, outside the limits of our present investigation and I have referred to it only that the reader might not receive a quite mistaken impression that Leo Nikolaevitch was lacking in that courageous joy in life affecting all around him, which, on the contrary, he possessed in the highest degree.[31]

---

[31]As I am touching upon the general mood of Leo Nikolaevitch's spiritual life, I foresee that the extracts I have made from his diaries and letters will in many readers arouse a feeling of regret that they have hitherto not had the opportunity of reading this precious material in its entirety. And therefore I think it needful to state that the principal obstacles to the continuation of the series of issues of Tolstoy's diaries, begun several years ago, and to the systematic publication of all his writings, are now happily

APPENDIX II

The personality of Leo Nikolaevitch's wife, Sofya Andreyevna, is connected in the closest way with the account I have given of his leaving home. I have consequently been compelled to touch upon her relations with her husband. While describing the agonising sufferings to which Leo Nikolaevitch was subjected in his family circle, I have to my regret been forced to state a great deal which appears as an attack upon the character and behaviour of his wife. And therefore, to prevent any misunderstandings on the part of readers with regard to my personal relations with her, I wish to speak out openly upon the subject.

It would perhaps have been natural for me, as a friend of Leo Nikolaevitch's, to feel bitterness and hostility towards the person who had been for him such a heavy cross during the last thirty years of his life. And it would be natural for the reader to suppose that under the influence of such feelings I could not be free from

overcome, and the first complete edition of all Tolstoy's works is at the present time being zealously prepared for the press.

prejudice in regard to Sofya Andreyevna, and could not help, even against my will, laying the colour on thick in describing her deficiencies. There will no doubt be ill-wishers who will say that, moved by resentment, I find a satisfaction in laying bare in an exaggerated form the mistakes and failings of a person who caused me much suffering. But in spite of the naturalness of such suppositions, they would in the present case be mistaken. In reality my attitude to Leo Nikolaevitch's wife is quite different.

First of all, as in Leo Nikolaevitch's lifetime I never forgot, so after the death of both of them I never can forget, that Sofya Andreyevna was his wife, i.e. occupied quite an exceptional position in regard to him, and for the first half of their life together was the person nearest to him in the world. This circumstance alone has inspired, and still inspires, a peculiar strictness toward myself in my behaviour to her and circumspection in my judgments of her. Moreover, having been a close witness of the wonderfully loving solicitude with which Leo Nikolaevitch behaved to his wife, never losing hope of the possibility of her spiritual awakening, I could not on my side help being infected by this attitude, at least so far as not to feel ill-will or prejudice against her.

Apart from that, I do not on principle acknowledge a man's right to judge another. The character and behaviour of this or the other person depends on so many external and internal circumstances for which the person is not in the least responsible; and the most secret region in our inner consciousness, in which we really are answerable to our own conscience, is so entirely beyond the reach of any outside eye that we have neither the power nor the right to judge any but ourselves. In relation to anyone else we can judge only their actions, laying completely aside, as not within our competence, the question of the degree of their responsibility for committing them. With this point of view every censure, irritation, or vexation with anyone, to say nothing of wrath or revenge, appears merely as the sign of our own imperfection, against which, when looked upon as such, it is easier to struggle than when such feelings are regarded as legitimate.

In view of these two circumstances, though I have, willy-nilly, in the present work to exhibit Sofya Andreyevna in an unfavourable light, I have not done so from personal ill-will to her, nor in a spirit of censure, but simply through the necessity of giving a faithful picture of what Leo Nikolaevitch had to endure.

I know that many will fail to understand my true motives and will severely censure me. I resign myself to this in advance. But I confess it grieves me, grieves me deeply, that by this present book I shall be bound to cause pain to those members of Leo Nikolaevitch's family who are still alive and who are nearest to him—his children. An old friend of their father's, I have always been conscious of being a friend of the family as well, and I naturally attach particular value to good relations with them. If they feel bitter against me, I beg them to believe that, whether mistakenly or not, I have, in any case, sincerely felt myself morally bound to act in the way I have acted, for reasons set forth in the Introduction. I beg them also to consider that the present publication of the truth I knew about their father's family life was, so to speak, forcibly wrung from me by all the untruths on the subject which for many years were persistently circulated all over the world, both in speaking and writing, by their own mother and their two brothers, Ilya Lvovitch and Leo Lvovitch. These two made it a kind of profession to give public lectures on the subject. Quite recently I came across, in one of the most popular foreign newspapers, the Paris Figaro, a series of articles by Leo Lvovitch

Tolstoy in which he strives to cover the memory of his father with shame and ignominy, in contradistinction to that of his mother, whose image he idealises till it becomes utterly distorted. He is so careless with the facts that, under the influence of his notorious envy and enmity for his father, he tells absolute untruths about him and definitely slanders him, though perhaps without meaning to do so. Such pernicious attacks upon Leo Nikolaevitch made in the world's Press by some of his nearest relatives give me reason to hope that his other relatives will not be surprised when they find, as their father's champion upon the same arena, one of his most intimate friends, who is able to speak more freely concerning the relations between their parents than those who are naturally constrained by the bonds of blood relationship.

It goes without saying that Sofya Andreyevna, like everyone else, had her virtues and her defects, but at the same time it will be readily understood that if Leo Nikolaevitch was reduced to the necessity of leaving her, it was not her good qualities which drove him to it. And therefore, in describing the causes of his departure, I have inevitably been forced to dwell upon the negative sides of her character.

In this brief narrative exclusively devoted to one definite event in the life of Leo Nikolaevitch and the internal and external circumstances connected with that event, I have not made it my aim to draw a general and complete picture of the characters of Leo Nikolaevitch and Sofya Andreyevna. The limited range of my special task laid upon me the necessity of keeping strictly within the limits of those of their characteristics and peculiarities which in one way or another threw a direct light upon the incident described. There could be no question of an all-round and to any extent exhaustive account of the characters of those persons, apart from the fact that such a task is far beyond my capacity. The most important and perhaps the most difficult aspect of the task which actually lay before me consisted in exhibiting in their full force the circumstances which in the end compelled Leo Nikolaevitch to take his final step, with perfect truthfulness, exaggerating nothing, of course, but at the same time concealing nothing from false delicacy. This I have tried to do as conscientiously, carefully and truthfully as I can. Though I might from the natural perhaps, but in the present case misplaced, sensibility have smoothed over the extremes of Sofya Andreyevna's behaviour, and have softened the real character of her attitude to Leo Nikolaevitch, yet in doing that I should have deprived the motives of his departure of reasonable basis and inevitability, and should have set forth Leo Nikolaevitch's impulses in a more or less distorted form—and that, of course, was inadmissible.

Even in the lifetime of Sofya Andreyevna Tolstoy I did at one time entertain the idea of publishing the truth about Leo Nikolaevitch's leaving home in her interests. I cherished the hope that from such a truthful account she might derive some conception of how much Leo Nikolaevitch suffered at her hands, how he struggled with himself, how self-sacrificingly he returned her good for evil, how persistently, in spite of everything, he believed in the divine spark in her soul, and how he rejoiced and was touched at the slightest gleam of that spark. And who knows, I said to myself, perhaps such a presentation before her eyes of what really happened, in contradistinction to the fantastic inventions with which she screened the truth from herself—perhaps this truthful picture of what Leo Nikolaevitch really did endure, might help her in time to recognise the truth, to come to herself, and to become one in soul with him who loved her so that he laid down his soul for her?

But at the time I did not decide to do this, and now I do not regret it. Apart from any external influences, there is no doubt that after Leo Nikolaevitch's death there appeared at times a certain inner softening in Sofya Andreyevna, though only of brief duration. So it was, for instance, immediately after his death, when, in the presence of several persons, she repeated in spiritual agonies that she had been the cause of his death. And though a prolonged period followed after it during which she displayed, at least in words, her former indifference or even hostility to Leo Nikolaevitch, yet before her own death, as those near her relate, she again expressed regret for the wrong she had done him. And if outwardly she repented but little, yet who can say what were her thoughts and reflections in her soul, and especially what passed in her consciousness during those dying hours and minutes when man, cut off from communication with those around him, in complete solitude before his Maker, knows that he is departing this life?

And though as she left this world Sofya Andreyevna carried with her the answer to this question, nevertheless we have no grounds for denying the possibility that the cherished hope which Leo Nikolaevitch never lost, that sooner or later she would be one with him in spirit, was realised at last before her death. Let us, too, look with a spirit of love and compassion upon the errors, the defects and the spiritual limitations of the companion of Leo Nikolaevitch's life. But at the same time let us boldly look the truth in the face, in no way softening the magnitude of the sufferings endured by Leo Nikolaevitch by concealing the true attitude of his wife to him, or by depicting her behaviour in a softened light. If we keep in mind the great divine love with which he loved her soul, then in face of the naked truth we shall not condemn, but shall sincerely compassionate, her whose destiny it was to serve as the instrument of his severest trials. And we shall understand that those trials which in the end exhausted Leo Nikolaevitch's physical forces and brought about his death were obviously needful to the manifestations in him of the fullness of spiritual strength received from him by God.